P9-ECJ-279

MEDIUM HERO

AND OTHER STORIES

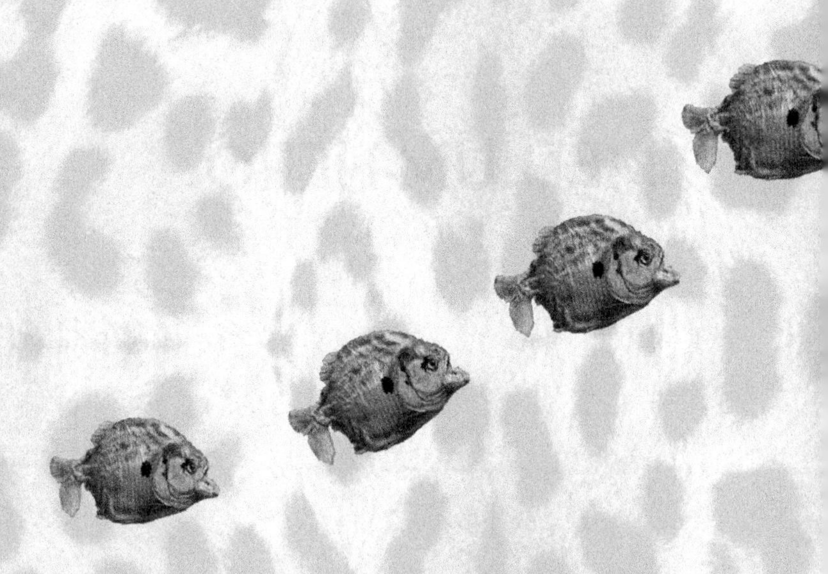

TURNER
PUBLISHING COMPANY

MEDIUM HERO

AND OTHER STORIES

Korby Lenker

Turner Publishing Company
424 Church Street • Suite 2240 • Nashville, Tennessee 37219
445 Park Avenue • 9th Floor • New York, New York 10022

www.turnerpublishing.com

Medium Hero and Other Stories

Cover image: Korby Lenker
Cover design: Scapati and Maddie Cothren
Book design: Glen Edelstein

Library of Congress Cataloging-in-Publication Data

Lenker, Korby.
[Short stories. Selections]
Medium hero and other stories / Korby Lenker.
pages cm
ISBN 978-1-68162-507-2 (pbk.) -- ISBN 978-1-68162-374-0 (hardback)
I. Title.
PS3612.E536A6 2015
813'.6--dc23
2015030300

Printed in the United States of America
14 15 16 17 18 19 0 9 8 7 6 5 4 3 2 1

FOR REV. BARBARA DAVENPORT

CONTENTS

MEDIUM HERO

AND OTHER STORIES

1. CAT LADY

I HAVE BEEN SPENDING too much time alone. Not alone. In the company of a cat. Which is worse.

Men who spend their waking hours walled off in some alley of the Self can at least claim the quiet dignity that accompanies true solitude. Beards may grow long, teeth brown, but a man in isolation has at least a chance at virtue.

I, however, am in love with a fuzzy white kitten, and, in the throes of some austere and worthy crisis of mind and heart, will suddenly scoop the animal up like an adoring mother and whisper into its ear one of ten nicknames I've made up. "My sweet Squee. Don't you *ever* leave me!" Poking the wet nose with an enthusiastic forefinger. A deep scratch between the shoulder blades. The animal's cross-eyed smile sending a wave of pleasure through me. Disgusting.

Sometimes these reveries last five minutes or more and find me splaying the helpless creature out on the couch, pushing his long white fur the wrong direction (does he like that?), letting him bite my hand, delighting in the tiny, stinging teeth pressed into the soft flesh of my outstretched palm. Scolding him in the ridiculous high-pitched voice. "*No!* Who's a bad kitty? *Fooface!*"

It is difficult to submerge oneself with any sincerity into questions involving the trajectory of peaceful relations in the Middle East or the future of literature in a technologically obese society when a prancing kitten decides your pinky might be a mouse and leaps over your laptop to pounce. Somehow an entire paragraph self-deletes. "My naughty Littlefat!" I hear myself say.

It wasn't always this way. From the perspective of true, steel-jawed manhood, I am a pale gadfly where once I was a gladiator.

Yes there was a time I was more brave.

A brief and incomplete accounting of my heroic deeds to date:

On the occasion of my twenty-ninth birthday and in the company of three drunk friends, I took hold of an electric fence, on purpose. The force of the shock knocked me backwards into the street and afterward made my hand twitch involuntarily for five minutes.

Three days after Sept 11 in 2001, I hitchhiked from Anchorage, Alaska, to Seattle, Washington, across the tundra and down the Al-Can Highway. Two thousand five hundred miles. It took four days. I carried a can of bear repellant with me. I spent a night in jail for traveling over international lines without a passport.

During college, under the spell of an imagined spiritual crisis, I spent an entire spring break walking alone through a desert in southern Utah with only a gallon of water and six oranges. I slept on the bare earth.

These are the things you do when possessed by an urgent and unclear need to demonstrate your grit to yourself and God and anyone else who would care to watch.

But now, in my gravity-succumbing thirties, I'm all ice cream and kitty cats. What happened?

I decide to reach out to a true friend.

I am a cat lady.

She texts back.

Everyone who knows you saw it coming.

I go for a walk. I reflect. The crisp bronze leaves of fallen autumn rustle under my feet like radio static. The light lays flat in the grey sky, shadowless.

I wonder: is it better to stay soft, to keep to the foothills of life, to watch football on Saturday afternoon eating too many nachos with your sweater-wearing friends? Or is it better to be a wild-eyed, stuttering prophet in scratchy sackcloth?

There was a time I felt like my path led to sackcloth. But then I found out I like beautiful things too much. A worn-in acoustic guitar. A well-wrought sentence cleaved of unnecessaries. A pretty girl.

I walk along a busy street. Cars pass beside me; only half the headlights are on. That twilight hour when not everyone is doing the same thing.

Have I abandoned my true calling? Am I a spiritual fat man? Am I just a random person on planet earth groping his way through make-believe and mystery like everyone else?

Sure, I could live in the desert, but there is no special virtue to eating bugs, especially when a sushi restaurant is in walking distance.

Sushi.

I call my friend Jacob and ask him to join me for dinner. He says yes. I keep walking.

Over California rolls and pints of Sapporo, I catch him up. The cat thing. The former glory of unreflective masculinity. I ask him what he thinks.

"Dude, you're probably gay," he offers. "I mean, you dress great."

I cast a quick glance down. Denim jacket, antique white cotton button-down, plaid madras bow tie, matching leather belt and shoes. Fair enough.

"I can see why you might say that, and, well, I don't want to sound defensive, but I don't like dudes."

"Have you tried 'em?"

"What do you mean?"

Jacob shrugs. "I didn't think I liked sushi. Then I tried it." He pushes a section of rainbow roll into his mouth. "I love sushi!"

I weigh his words and stir wasabi into the soy sauce. "I made out with a dude once. I didn't like it."

"What didn't you like about it?"

"Uh, everything. Whiskers. Gross. He was a dude. Dudes are disgusting. I like girls. They're soft and they smell nice and they're delicate. Who wouldn't like a girl?"

"I don't know man. I'm not the gay one." He looks at me and smiles and eats the whole pile of pickled ginger off his plate in one bite.

I let Jacob pay for dinner. We shake hands. He walks back to his car and says over his shoulder, "You're fine. It's okay to like cats."

"Mark Twain loved cats!" I shout back.

I stand on the sidewalk in my denim finery and consider his words. "It's not the cat," I finally say to no one. I turn and start walking back home.

The sidewalk I'm on follows a road that bends evasively around a college campus. As I walk, a handsome twenty-something with a short black haircut steps from the front door of a Thai restaurant, a pretty honey-blonde girl right behind him. They fall in step in front of me. For awhile they walk side by side. Then suddenly the fingers of the boy's right hand make the smallest reaching motion, and all at once they are holding hands, in the not-quite-all-the-way style of familiar lovers. A casual intersection of hearts and fingers.

We all continue this way—lovers and witness—for a hundred or so feet, until the couple reaches their car.

The car chirps, the hands separate, and the girl walks alone to the passenger side. The boy lifts the latch on the driver's door and slides inside. The passenger door slams shut, the lights come on, and just as I walk past, the car pulls out into the street and disappears.

I consider one of my more recent romances.

The bullet points: young girl, fair-faced, overtly indifferent to my presence one way or another, but with a certain whispered affection that came in unlikely moments like a surprise. For whatever reason, this is the kind of girl I like, and like her I did. I read to her aloud from my favorite books. I rubbed her feet. I made her breakfast. I wrote a song for her.

What happened? I started to be myself is what happened. Too excitable, too many opinions, too much thinking about everything, just too *much*. She didn't care for the sum total.

The phone in my pocket vibrates. I pull it out and look at the screen. My true friend. It says:

Put down the cat I am calling you.

As I'm reading the text the phone rings and I answer it. I say: "Another thing that makes me mad. Dudes don't open doors anymore. Bad manners everywhere."

"It's worse than that," comes the sharpened voice, "I hear they stopped teaching cursive in elementary school."

"Hilarious. Take me seriously or I'm hanging up."

"Honey. It's impossible to take you seriously. You wear a bow tie and I bet at this moment your belt matches your shoes. Am I right?"

I don't say anything.

"Also you like cats. Who likes cats?"

"Lonely people."

"Barf. Everyone is lonely. Write us a song."

"I'm going to write a song about good manners."

"Do it. God knows we need you to show us the way. You're our last hope, Obi-Wan."

"Why are you in such a good mood?"

"You know why? I'm talking to you, loverboy. Look," she says, "I can tell you're having one of your flights of fancy. You've probably been walking around your neighborhood for the last hour looking at leaves and thinking about whichever girl it is you're currently hung up on. Somewhere along the way, something caught your eye – some small detail – and you've spun it like a pizza dough into some universal truth about the nature of being alive in the twenty-first century. No doubt you're feeling depressed, misunderstood, etc. How close am I?"

I kick at some leaves. "Why again did you call?"

"To cheer you up! It's not like your goddamn cat's gonna do that."

I push my hand through my hair. "It's not working."

"Of course it's working. You love this. Someone reached out and scooped your furry ass up and is scratching you under your ugly chin. Messed up as it is, this is the way you like to be loved. I swear I can hear you purring through the phone."

"You are annoying and I do not like you."

“Stick it,” she says. “My kids are yelling at me. I’ll talk to you later.”

She hangs up.

I round the last corner to my house. Night is in full bloom. Darkness leans on my street like an old man. I walk up to my house and pause. A warm yellow light spills out of the two front windows into the yard. In the rightmost frame, the unmistakable silhouette of my cat stands in the sill.

2. DEAR WILLOW REEDER

YOU WERE MY OLD PIANO teacher, and now you are dead. You were killed yesterday in a car crash in my hometown of Twin Falls, Idaho. My dad called and left a message saying Happy Easter, and oh your piano teacher died. I called him back and found out it happened at about 3PM, mountain time. You pulled out in front of a small pickup, which then slammed into your driver's side door and lifted your Camry three feet into the air and hefted it far into the sagebrush. Relaying this, my dad wondered aloud if you're another reason why people in their eighties maybe shouldn't drive.

Wherever there is death there is irony, dear Willow, and in that respect you did not disappoint. For one, you were killed coming home from a mortuary. You had just finished playing the organ at someone else's funeral, rubbing the foot pedals with your spindly legs and stocking feet. I think it's strange and merciful and a little funny you didn't know your life was about to come to a violent end. "The Dirge You Play Just Might Be Your Own," is a song title I just thought of.

The other irony, the sad one, is that you were newly married, and, in my dad's words, "as giddy as a young girl." I remember your first husband Fran as a kindly old man with a white duster mustache who smoked cigarettes under the carport while I played scales. Fran died, and a year ago you re-married and were happy with your new man. You knew true love twice. But it's a sad thing when love is cut short, and even if you and yours were old, your love was not. You were eighty-two and yet you managed to work a little tragedy into your closing act. So of course I am proud of you for this.

I have some things to say to you, Willow. I have kept them to myself for almost ten years, but now that you are dead I think it's time you heard them. One is we both know you were a bad teacher. You probably know why but let me spell it out for you: you were indulgent, and by that I mean you didn't care what I played. I believe you had no special love for Bach or Brahms or anyone really, you just wanted me to play something, even if it was "Wind Beneath My Wings." I still can't believe you taught me that song. What's worse is that whenever I think of my piano lessons – even though there were eight years of them and a hundred pieces – it's that song I think of. My whole musical youth is captured in a single saccharine Bette Midler ballad. Willow, this is embarrassing to me. Since you are no more and therefore omnipotent to a degree, I hope you understand why.

But that's only part of it. Okay so fine, you were

a bad teacher. I want you to know that after I went to college and actually learned a thing or two about music, I thought of you with genuine disdain. I felt like I had to play catch-up on everything I had missed. That I could have been so much farther ahead. I think I may have even sullied your name to a few empathetic girlfriends. But then I wandered from jazz to classical music to bluegrass to this weird sort of everything-music I make now, and I see the gift your kindly mediocrity was to me: you gave me permission to be self-directed. You never imposed, and so I never knew music as anything but a pleasure. You didn't really teach me much, but at that baby grand in your house on Fillmore Street in Twin Falls, you allowed something precious and rare to take shape in my little eight-year-old heart. Namely, that it was okay to be delighted by whatever delighted me.

Sure, my parents could have hired one of the Mormon teachers in town to scold me into submission, but they didn't. They hired you. And you let me play "Wind Beneath My Wings," and "I Heard it Through the Grapevine," and "The Entertainer," and "Fur Elise" after I heard it in the McDonald's commercial. I played what made me happy, which is what I still do.

So, that's why I'm writing you, Willow. You are a brand new angel after eighty-two years, and I am thankful for the part of your life you gave to me. Happy Easter.

3. RAT'S DUDE

HERE WAS SOMETHING that happened to me one night during my last tour:

I was in the high California desert, east of Los Angeles, past the part of the highway where rows and rows of windmills spin lazy-like in the hot wind. I had just played a show at a small, kindly place in Joshua Tree. And because I didn't know anyone around there and had nowhere else to go, I thought I might stay at a motel across the street.

While I was packing up my guitar, I asked the bartender about it. Was it an okay place? She said yes, except that the last unit on the ground floor was home to a registered sex offender. I asked which room it was, and she said I would know because he slept with his door open.

So it was kind of disturbing when I pulled my grey Volvo station wagon into the dusty parking lot of this rundown hotel and saw right off the door she was talking about. It was wide open and I could see the blue light coming from inside. I wondered what kind of TV show a rapist watches.

I was feeling pretty curious so before I took my stuff out of the car I walked over in my flip flops, maybe fifteen feet from the doorway, until I could sort of see the TV. But it was at a funny angle, and I couldn't really make it out. Then I thought to listen because sometimes that way you can tell, like if it's *Wheel of Fortune* it's obvious because of the sound the spinning wheel makes.

I listened but that's when I noticed there was no sound. Whoever was inside was watching the TV on silent. Hmm that's odd, I thought.

At this point I really wanted to know what show he liked, so I walked to the doorway. "Maybe he's not even here," I said to myself. He could have walked to the store to get a beer and left his door open because who would dare to walk into a rapist's dumpy hotel room at night?

So I just went square up to the doorway and looked inside. But that was the wrong guess, because he wasn't out getting a beer. He was sitting on the bed, watching his TV with the mute on. He was a sort of fat forty-something and mostly bald with grey-brown hair growing on the sides and back of his head. And really big, wild-looking eyebrows. And, I kid you not, he was wearing a wife-beater that was supposed to be white but wasn't even close now. Like Bruce Willis' shirt halfway through *Die Hard.*

Anyway, he looked up at me, kind of distractedly. I thought two things in that moment. One was,

"I think something weird is about to happen." And the other was, "Who watches South Park without the sound?"

Without alarm he said, "How much?"

So I said "twenty." I don't know why I said it. I just thought it would be interesting to go with the flow.

And he said, "What do you mean 'twenty'? You're Rat's dude, or what?"

And I thought, "Stop being stupid, Simon. This man has been to prison."

So I said, "Actually, I don't know why I just said that. I don't know who Rat is. I just came over because I don't have a TV in my room and I was wondering what was on right now." It was a lie flat out, because I hadn't even checked into the motel yet. But I was improvising and didn't know what else to say.

I thought he would probably say something rude at that point. Instead, he just said, "Nice shirt." Which made me feel self-conscious. But it was a nice shirt after all, white with flowers and sequins on it, so I said, "Thanks."

"You gay or something?" was his next question. Also understandable, considering the embroidery.

"Well, no, but you're not the first person to ask me that. I think I'm a metrosexual."

"Whatever that is, fag," is what he said. But he laughed when he said it. Not really a mean laugh or anything, just a laugh-for-the-sake-of-laughing laugh. So I laughed, too.

He shifted his weight on the bed, reaching into

a dirty styrofoam cooler. "Wanna beer?" he asked indifferently.

"Um, okay." He threw me a can.

Then he got up, saying, "I feel like smokin'." He walked past me and sat down on a cracked white plastic chair that was resting on the cement sidewalk outside his door. There was a yucky-looking red bucket next to the chair. I saw it had three cigarette butts in it. "Hmm that's tidy," I thought.

There was nowhere else to sit, so I sat down on the cement on the other side of the doorway with my back against the wall and looked out over the parking lot. It was a perfectly still desert night, warm and dry. I popped the beer. It was ice cold. I was happy, because this was an Unusual Event.

"That your car?" he asked. Mine was the only car in the lot.

"Yep."

"What year is it?"

"An '85."

"My dad had one of those when I was a kid. An old one. '67. Cool car. Slow as hell but sturdy like a plank. You know anything about cars?"

"No. I used to, kind of. When I was younger, I was really into my Volkswagen bus. Did my own tune-ups and oil changes and stuff. Once I even replaced the engine. But then I started playing music, and I don't like getting my hands dirty now." Hmm, that sounded snobby.

He took a drag, paused, blew a long stream of

translucent smoke into the parking lot. "Don't blame you. I work sometimes at the wrecking yard down in Palm Springs. Dirty work. Pulling brake drums off totaled Saabs, windshields, whatever. Look at this." He held up his thumb. There was no fingernail on it. Just a lot of meaty-looking skin. It looked painful.

"Did that six months ago, getting the passenger seat out of a Lexus. Still fuckin' hurts."

"Looks it," I said. I took a big sip of beer. He smoked.

We didn't say anything for about a minute. Then he said, "I love this goddamn desert." He put the cigarette to his lips, and the orange ball grew bright.

"What do you love about it?" I asked. I wanted to know.

He blew the smoke between compressed lips. It took a long time. He moved his wild eyebrows up and down and looked out at the parking lot. There was no sound except for the streetlight a block away that clicked when it changed from red to green.

"It's quiet," he said eventually.

I took the last swallow of my beer. Just then a car pulled up, an old sand-colored Camaro, from out of nowhere it seemed like. It stopped at an angle in the middle of the gravel parking lot and the engine shut off.

"That's probably Rat's dude."

"Well, thanks for the beer," I said.

"You take it easy, buddy."

I set the empty can on the sidewalk and stood up

and walked across the lot to the motel office. I tried to make out the driver of the car, but the windows were tinted and no one got out. As I reached the glass door of the office, I heard behind me the latch pop and a car door swing open, but the moment had passed. I didn't turn around.

It only took five minutes to make arrangements with the clerk, but while I was inside I heard a car door slam and the Camaro rumble to life. Rat's dude punched the gear and sped out of the lot, tossing gravel.

4. CATFISH

Come pick me up

IS WHAT THE TEXT SAID. No punctuation. No please. A simple sentence. The simplest. No, not quite a sentence. It had no formal end. So, not a sentence, then. A command. Or maybe a straightforward request. No, he knew her. A command. An imperative.

Come pick me up

Drop what you're doing and come and get me. Come get me and take me from this place where I am to the place I hope to be. I may have something in mind, or you may be required to furnish one or more ideas, depending on how good your first idea is. I may feel like a beer or I may feel like a coffee or I may feel like something I haven't thought of and won't think of until you suggest it. So, have a few ideas ready. Also, I may need to change my mind at any moment, so don't get too comfortable.

Simon was already brushing his teeth. People who knew Simon knew he only did this on special occasions. And this was one of them. A special occasion. He was going to see the girl.

Come pick me up

And I will reward you with some of the benefits of my presence. Those benefits are as follows: I will permit you to attempt to make me laugh, to dig deep into your repertoire of wit and folly, spin out one of your far-fetched stories while I listen, perhaps only distractedly. If you are successful, you will have your reward. You will see me smile. You will watch my eyes twinkle like distant stars, dance around like gypsies. And you will be glad because you'll know that they are dancing despite themselves. I dare you to try. Come pick me up.

I believe I will

The season summer, the night hot, the car heading south, Simon finished the text and returned his hands to the wheel to wait out the red light. All four windows were down, not because the night was pleasant but because he had no air conditioning.

The skin on Simon's face was shiny at the forehead, his hair a little discouraged from the balloon of humidity that permeated his immediate environment and the thousand or so miles around it. He examined the wilted hairs drooping in the rear view mirror and absentmindedly pushed them back up from his face, giving them a chance. They looked a little braver. He returned his attention to the scene beyond the windshield. The light changed from red to green.

As he encouraged the car through its transition from second to third gear, Simon took stock of his general situation, and was, at the moment, pleased. The girl he was about to see was the girl he loved. *Loved.* He didn't say it lightly.

He was a silver salmon from the cold waters of the Pacific Northwest, and he had been swimming a long time, looking. He had swum in all the blue grey seas of the world, in choppy water and smooth, looking for one who would swim with him. Not just swim, but swim with him in the *deep.* He had been around, had run with exotic clownfish and common trout, and there was something in them all that he liked, but nothing he loved. Most all the fish he knew hung near the surface where the food was easy. He liked to dive.

He neared another light. It clicked red. As he slowed down, the car shuddered like an old man pushing a walker. Funny old car. The light changed while he watched, and he turned left onto the boulevard.

And then a year ago he had found this girl, this southern catfish. This blue-eyed rarity of a creature who, behind her smooth skin and slow gaze, kept hidden a heart which knew no bottom. He had found her, he had seen the heart, and it was from that moment forever impossible the world could be anything but new. The water through which he moved grew warm. The shimmering tendrils of light now reached below the surface, deeper, down to the dark water to meet him where he was. He had found her, and the scales on his own skin changed color. They were always silver, lustrous, arrogant even, but this girl, this slippery catfish of a girl, had turned him blue. He was humbled. He would do anything.

Kay. I'm here

A period. She was feeling lighthearted, sweet. The car began to move imperceptibly faster, like a magnet was involved.

He turned onto her street. Oh yes, ideas. He thought it over. He was going to suggest a long walk. She was no hipster. She liked to walk. She wore Chacos.

He wheeled into the driveway of the house she shared. He turned the key and the engine shuddered and died. He cut the lights. He looked again in the mirror. The hairs lay down in defeat. No matter, she knew what he looked like.

Twenty feet to the front door. Porch light on, a cloud of dizzy moths. He looked through the screen, pulled it open and entered, saying her name with a question mark at the end.

"Just a minute!"

The lights inside were off. He stood in the living

room and extended his arms, making a cross shape in the dark. Airing himself out in the name of consideration.

He closed his eyes and took a deep breath, for no real reason other than he liked to do that. She must have come in at exactly the right second because he only got through one breath before her voice filled up the room like a breeze.

"What are you doing, Simon?"

"Oh, you know, um . . ."

"Are you airing yourself because you stink?"

"No, of course not."

"Let me smell."

"I have nothing to hide."

He remembered then to open his eyes. She had turned on the light. The light came from behind, silhouetting her head and surrounding it with an imperceptible halo. He laughed out loud at the perfection of the gesture. She was the prettiest fish in the widest part of the warmest ocean. Her hair was down, was everywhere. Cascading was the word. He looked at her feet. Chacos.

She took two steps toward him. She wrinkled her nose.

"We should probably go for a walk," she said. "That way I won't have to smell you."

He looked at her, smiling like a crook, like a pirate.

"Whatever you say, catfish."

She cast him a wry glance, took another step forward. He could smell her perfume.

There was a pause while the ocean refilled.

She tilted her head slightly to the left, and then she advanced a little more, and then she moved toward him until her cheek was just under his chin. He felt her work the cheek a little more deeply into that place on his neck. She wrapped her arms around him, beneath his arms, and he wrapped his arms around her, over her shoulders, and he pulled her into him. A wave broke through the room and twisted their fingers and hair together like seaweed and washed the furniture out the front door, and the light from the lamp shivered in the reflected pools of seawater that lay at their feet while the warm blue ocean drained away into the night.

It's good to see you.

5. FOR APRIL

ONCE UPON A TIME there was a young girl who worked in an office in a small city in America.

From the outside, she looked very much like the other girls who worked in her office. She bought her clothes at places like H&M, wore her hair up or down depending on her mood, read *Rolling Stone* on her breaks. In some ways, she was not special. She drove a Subaru. Lived in a little apartment with hardwood floors. Went to church occasionally.

But there was something behind the girl's eyes that made children in strollers reach up when their mothers pushed them by. It made small birds line up on the telephone wire outside her front door, made tall grasses lean toward her as she walked past.

What the girl had she didn't choose or even want, it was just there. I am a boy so I will never really know, but if I tried I would say she had an ache in her heart, that couldn't be healed. This was because it was the ache of the world, as ancient as sand and bottomless as the Black Sea. You think I am exaggerating, but I've seen the birds on the wire and I've seen the children reach out and I've seen the eyes that look like they are crying even when they are not.

On a recent Monday, the girl was driving back to her office from lunch. She was with one of her friends, a coworker with smooth olive skin and a friendly lisp. As she pulled up to the stoplight, she chanced to look over and saw a homeless man sitting under a shade tree. He had long black dreadlocks and one of them was tied around the others so as to make an enormous, cartoonish ponytail.

It was a fine spring day, and while she waited on the light, she watched him rummage around in a small backpack. Maybe for something to eat? She didn't know, but while she watched, he looked up and met her eyes. His smile was transparent. The girl instantly knew this man without knowing him. She smiled back. The light changed. She drove on and thought about the perfect spring day and him outside in the fresh air and her under the buzzing florescent lights.

On the following day, the weather was different. The fickle March wind carried a storm up from the gulf, and so all morning while checking emails in her cubicle, the girl listened to the windows rattle and felt the dull gloom of the day fill her chest. At lunch she went out again. This time, her olive-skinned friend drove, and as they talked about the little pleasures and frustrations of the morning, she looked out the window and felt glad to be warm.

They were driving down the same street as the day before when she saw the man again. How strange! There he was, walking down the sidewalk with that backpack on, his long black dreadlocks wrapped up in a grey hoodie that made his head look swollen like an alien. It was raining steadily, but there was a lilt in his step. Behind the sea-green eyes that looked out the window, there stirred in her heart a feeling of kinship for this man and his bold spirit, which would not be defeated by a grey day and a steady rain.

While she ate, she talked with her friend about status updates and funny tweets, but her heart was wrapped up in a wet hoodie, and the quiet ache made her afternoon work go slowly.

The next day, the storm changed from blowing rain to freezing sleet. Her friend had called in sick and so she drove to lunch alone. She thought she would have a Happy Meal, so she pulled into the McDonald's and walked across the parking lot. The sleet was so fine it looked like mist but felt like tiny pinpricks on her skin.

As she was waiting in line, she looked around the McDonald's and suddenly drew a sharp breath because there he was, the man with the dreadlocks and the backpack. He was sitting at the window table, eating french fries one at a time. She watched him for a second and thought about the thrice-born coincidence, and then she noticed something she hadn't seen before. He was eating with one hand. She looked closely and saw that his right arm was good, but his left arm tapered to an unnatural, early end, well before the place where his wrist should be.

She watched him finish eating, and her heart flooded with the secret ache. He stood up and fumbled with the backpack, trying once and again to fit the funny-shaped arm through the strap. Something about this small struggle inside an empty McDonald's struck her as heroic and unjust, and she felt embarrassed tears fill up her eyes.

The man and his dreadlocks got the backpack on at last. He carried the tray in his good hand toward the garbage can to throw it away. As he walked past, their eyes met. He paused and asked, "Do I know you?" And the girl felt ridiculous because she was crying for a stranger in a public place, so she shook her head no.

He said, "Well. You are a beautiful girl indeed. Is your name Becky? Because if it's Becky, that would be too good to be true." The girl's name was not Becky, but she shook her head yes anyway. He smiled. They had an ancient moment, him with the tray in his good hand and her in line for a Happy Meal, and he finally said, "You have a good day Miss Becky. It was very nice to meet you." He pushed open the glass door with his good hand and walked into the frozen mist.

She got her Happy Meal and set it aside and put her head down on the table and let secret tears drop from her eyes into a salty puddle she hid with her arms. It was the homeless man's useless hand and his kind heart. It was the sleet and the terrible indifference of this broken-hearted life and the birds outside her door and the children in their strollers and the tall grasses and the ache in her chest which would not heal and the steady smile she would wear in a few minutes when she went back to work and answered the phone.

6. BIRTHDAY CARDS

I WAS IN A MOOD. It was late, very late, and I was walking through a quiet neighborhood in Green Hills. Not walking, cantering. Do people canter? I was going somewhere quickly, and I was in a mood.

A car drove past and flashed its brights. I must have looked like a jogger. Maybe someone who came home from the night shift and wanted a little exercise while the air was cool. White T-shirt, off-brand grey shorts, red headband I found on the ground one day and washed and now wore all the time. I was bright, visible, harmless.

Not quite a jogger, though. In my right hand I held a staple gun purchased a few days before. It was silver, heavy for its size. In my left was a stack of 3 x 5 cards with little sayings scrawled on them in my bad handwriting. Sayings, maxims I had written down. Not many. Just some things I came up with a few minutes before over a late-night bourbon.

I was about to celebrate a birthday. Celebrate was not the word. I was in a mood. *People with enormous egos do not age gracefully.* That was one of the quotes, actually. The one on top.

I rounded the first corner by my house and ran up to a tree in the front yard of a two-story brick number with perfectly square windows and no eaves on the roof. Two trees out front. Sycamores? I wish I knew something about plant life. I chose the closer one. The loud pop from the staple gun made me flinch, but it was satisfying to see the card there at eye level, a bright golden rectangle in the streetlight. I imagined what it would look like in the morning when it was discovered by the owners of the house. What would they think? Students from the nearby university? Except Lipscomb was a good Christian school, and nice kids don't staple trees.

A gift, a birthday gift from me to them, a piece of harmless weirdness bestowed by the court jester of Green Hills to give them something to tell their coworkers about. *Nothing unpredictable ever happens anymore* was the next card. I do like a bit of irony.

I ran across the street to a dark yard with a handsome white birch that slanted off at a funny angle. Suddenly, I knew I would tag one tree in each lawn for six houses in a row, three on each side. It would be mass vandalism, a full-scale commercial campaign. It would be a communal experience. They would discuss it on the 4th of July, or whenever it is that neighbors get together.

There was the popping sound and the card fixed

there like a police notification. *Nothing unpredictable ever happens anymore.* Man, that is funny.

It only took about four minutes to do the other yards. One Bible verse, a few sayings by Nietzsche, some random stuff I made up, like *Bring back the divine right of kings* and *Entropy is the real enemy.* Nothing important, just a little bruising Bohemian advice, playful. I hoped the charm would not go unnoticed.

A dog started barking in one of the backyards. I quickened my pace. No need to get arrested; there was never a need. Ah, but sometimes it happened. But then it was just another story, and isn't that the point?

Anyway, it was sad. I had just left my house and already I was out of cards. One left. I knew which house this one was for.

There is a mansion about a mile from mine that must be the actual, physical counterpart to the cartoon mansion owned by Mr. Burns on *The Simpsons*. The columns, the endless sweeping yard, the gentle slope of the ground down and away from the magisterial front porch. The tall iron fence, ancient and impressive. How much did that fence cost? More than I've made in the ten years I've been a legal adult. Burnished glossy black iron that stood like an endless row of spears. Like a cartoon fence.

I walked, cantered, ran a little bit. Just off Granny White Pike, slight left, and I was there, standing before the spears, gazing uphill at the broad white columns turned yellow by the tasteful outdoor lighting. The trees, a dozen of them, scattered unevenly throughout the immaculate front yard. Were there dogs? I doubted it. Which is why I didn't hesitate to thrust my right foot in between two bars and lever myself in one smooth motion up and over the spears. I am from Idaho. I am athletic.

I landed with a quiet thump and reached back through the fence to grab my staple gun and index card. I looked up and took stock of my surroundings. Which tree?

The one closest to the house, of course.

As luck would have it, there was a small Japanese maple (I knew because of the purple leaves) just left of the front door. Perfect. I wanted whoever lived here, not their greenskeeper, to see the card. I wanted them to see it in the morning. The next morning.

I picked the side that faced the door and sent one staple into the little trunk with a loud pop.

Isn't this better than television?

Of course of course of course a light would go on upstairs. *Shit!* I turned and broke into full sprint mode, imagining Mr. Burns upstairs, shouting "Release the hounds!" But there were no hounds, just me clearing the fence and disappearing onto dark and friendly Tower Road. I could hear the echo of my own laughter bouncing off the surrounding brick houses. I am the youngest old man I know. Happy Birthday, Korby.

7. MEDIUM HERO

HE WISHED HE HAD a mental disease. At least then he would have an excuse. The burden of normalcy was the most unbearable part of all this.

Normal. He was depressingly normal. He was good at conversation. He could keep a job. He could show up to work on time. He paid rent. He more or less kept up with his bills. He had no real perversions, sexual or otherwise. All his addictions were mild and commonplace. The drinking wasn't too bad. He watched just enough TV to qualify for modern life. There was a good bit of him that could even be described as innocent. He liked kids. He was good with parents. Normal. The word sent a shudder through him.

He lay beneath the covers and stared up at the ceiling. It seemed to darken as he watched. He let his eyes go out of focus. It was going to be hard to get out of bed today.

Even though he had to pee, he lay there for a long time, trying to fall back asleep. He lay in a daze, dreaming a half-dream about his first job as a teenager, working for his dad at the mortuary. Mowing the lawn out in front of the mortuary. Washing the black hearse. Washing the hearse and imagining all the dead bodies it had carried. Scrubbing the black tires and washing the curtained windows of the hearse and imagining all the mourning people who followed behind in a parade of wailing grief because someone they loved had died and would never come back again, not in a million years. *Stop. You must stop.* Be brave. Brave people do things even when they cannot bear it. He must go do something. He would go to the post office. He could send something. That would be useful; yes, he would do that.

He watched himself put his clothes on. The same clothes he had been wearing for four days. He thought, that guy should think about wearing something different. People will notice. Then he laughed in his head because he was talking about himself. Maybe he did have a mental disease. No, he didn't. He was just being dramatic; plus, he couldn't think of what else to wear.

At last, the man who was him was fully clothed. Brown and brown and brown. Right down to his well-tied shoes. He walked across the room to hear the sound the shoes made on the wood. A clean clicking sound. That was good, it brought him back a little.

Now down the wooden stairs and more clicking and then pulling open the door. An icy wind touched him up and down. He had no coat, so he hurried out to the car and got in and started the engine and waited and thought of what to do after the post office. That was another problem. You always had to think of what to do next.

The engine warmed and the windshield cleared and little bits of snow fell down around the car like dead lice. Another day he would have noticed how pretty it all was. But today was a different kind of day. It was a tightrope day. He put the car in drive.

Maybe some music? After all, he was someone known to associate with musical things and people. Maybe it would help. He pushed the button. The song that came on was "Mad World", the *Donnie Darko* version. He had put it on a CD with some other songs that sounded like crazy hopelessness. Of all of them, "Mad World" is the song someone most likely plays before they shoot themselves in their car in the snow. He laughed because it was all so silly. He turned off the music and drove in silence to the post office. The car made a high-pitched whining sound because it was old.

This is what happened next.

He was driving like anyone would, at a normal speed in a normal way, when he wheeled the car into the parking lot of the post office. There was a man walking through the parking lot, making his way to the front door. A little girl, his daughter probably, was walking behind him ten or so feet. The man turned back toward his daughter to see where she was. And then he turned back around and looked through the windshield, straight into the eye of our boy dressed in brown and brown, and shouted, "Slow the fuck down!" It wasn't necessary. He was not driving fast, nor was the little girl in any danger. But the man was so angry.

That alone should not have been enough to hasten the descent that followed. Not enough on a normal day. But it pulled the string, and the sweater unraveled. The young driver paused, realizing that the man was going into the post office, and that he, too, was planning on going into the post office, and that he would have to stand behind him in line. But there was lice in the air and the world was pitching sideways and he couldn't at that moment bear the thought of spending ten minutes standing next to someone who had just yelled at him. It was not possible.

He could hear the sound of the sweater coming undone. A slipping sound. He put the car back in drive and pulled out onto the street, going nowhere.

He drove aimlessly, trying to think of what to do next. It was hard to think. The snow had turned to rain and then back to snow. He turned the music back on. "Mad World." It was the worst kind of day. It was bigger than a day.

The tightrope. He thought, I am getting what I asked for. He thought about all the times he had wished and prayed that he wouldn't ever become complacent. And here he was, getting what he wanted. In a way. But maybe this was different. Maybe this was something more than unsatisfied. To be unsatisfied implied there was a chance for advancement. And advancement implied hope. He didn't feel any of those things.

He drove on the freeway. He took an exit. He was lost.

At last he decided something. He would drive to his friend Jack's apartment. Jack would be out for the day. He could sit in that apartment in the quiet, rarified air, six stories up, and try to think of what to do next.

He drove like a robot. He felt like nothing.

He turned into the parking garage of a high-rise apartment building and steered his car into an empty space. He sat in the car seat for too long. The air grew cold around him. He had to move very deliberately to move at all.

Open the door.
Get out of the car.
Walk through the revolving door.
Scan the key thing.
Wait for the doors to open.
Push 6 on the elevator.
Scan the key thing again.
Wait for the doors to open.
Walk down the hall to the second door on the left.
Put the key into the lock and turn it.
Walk through the door.

He stopped at the threshold and looked inside. It was a fancy modern apartment with high ceilings and bamboo floors and the pleasant, fresh smell unique to wealthy people. Yes. He could rest for a moment and think.

He sat on the couch. There was a bottle of expensive scotch on the coffee table. He stood up and retrieved a tumbler from the cupboard and came back to the couch and poured a three fingered shot into the glass. He took a deep sip. It tasted like smoke.

To his left were two enormous windows spanning the wall from floor to ceiling. His mouth full of scotch, he looked through them at another modern high-rise apartment building, sullen in the darkening day. More slushy snow. It was late afternoon. The sky was a dead grey yawn opening overhead. He thought he could see teeth in the clouds.

He sat for a long time. *This is what is called true loneliness. I don't think I've known this feeling before. I have felt alone, but to be truly lonely, you need another feeling also. And that feeling is called hopelessness. Once you feel there is no hope for you, you can enter into that new room, the one with the heavy doors which close behind you and block out all the sound.*

There he was in this empty apartment, six stories up, with a blanket on his lap and stone in his chest. The grey-black sky and the slushy snow and the bamboo floors.

Suddenly, the phone rang. He looked down at it. It was someone he knew. A friend. He wanted to pick it up. His friend's pretty face was showing on the screen. He could picture her real face, holding the phone up to her ear, cheerful, checking in. He wanted to pick it up but he couldn't. What would he say? Hello, I'm thinking of being dead soon? Hello, I'm so lonely I want to throw up? No, that would never do. Even here, in this room with the heavy doors, he had his pride.

Mercifully, the phone stopped ringing. A new, louder silence settled in the room.

The cars on the freeway sounded far away. Everything was far away.

He walked over to the sliding glass door and opened it. Wind rushed in like a delighted child. He walked out onto the balcony.

He could think of it without fear. The ultimate show-stopper. The last bang. This vacuum of hopelessness was empowering. He walked through the glass door, carrying the scotch, and stood at the rail. He thought of the clips he had seen on the internet of people jumping off buildings. The internet had no shame. You could see anything you wanted, even people dying.

The snow and the grey-black, yawning, dead-man's sky and the smoky scotch and the breathless feeling of being stuck behind closed heavy doors even out here in the wind and heights.

The tightrope. This is what he had asked for. This is what he had driven across the country for. Away from his home, his family, his childhood. He was so far from home he would have to drive four straight days to get there. Home felt forever away.

He tipped the glass of scotch and watched a little spill out over the rail. At first it fell in a stream, but a few seconds later it broke up and hit the pavement in a splatter.

Randomly, he thought about the poet Robert Frost. Frost had said, "The only lost soul is the one who can't find himself a *gathering metaphor.*"

A gathering metaphor. Meaning, if you can find a pretty phrase for your misery, you might be able to survive. But if you can't, you're screwed.

He was out of ideas. He was screwed.

A hundred images blew through him like the wind on the balcony. Disconnected things from his childhood. The muskrat that he had spat on after he and his brother had trapped it in a cage in their backyard. The spit had landed in its eye and ran down its face like a tear, and then two minutes later it was dead because his brother shot it with a pistol. Jumping on the trampoline on a summer night in Idaho with his little sister. Her happy laugh, her simple happiness. His dad kneeling at the side of his bed when he had been sick, reading a story from the Bible and praying over him. The man he had seen die in a car accident on a deserted highway in Oregon. The wheezing sound the dying man had made, the death rattle. The advent candles on Christmas Eve, the low yellow light that had made his mother's face shine like a saint. His grandfather, the soft-spoken Nazarene preacher, standing over him at his wedding, pronouncing him man and wife in his shaky, careful voice. The divorce. The scraping sound he had heard when he stood before the judge and signed the papers that said *irretrievably broken*. The nights and nights and nights of music, for his friends and for people he didn't know and never would know. The loud music of the club, the soft music of the house concert. The staying up late at night trying to get that lick down.

He leaned out over the rail and dropped the tumbler into the street. The crash was surprisingly loud. No one saw.

He thought about it again. The thing he was thinking of. It was an act of cowardice, true. But also it wasn't. Not this way. It took some serious balls to throw yourself off a balcony into the street. How much easier it was, in a dull, aching way, to grow steadily older, put up with the sagging face and widening ass and estranged relationships that would come. It was easier to hold on than to let go. To let go, he thought. There should be a round of applause for the sheer bravery of the act.

But not every act. Taking pills was not heroic, no. Shooting yourself, maybe. Cutting your wrists, definitely. Throwing yourself off a building was somewhere between shooting and pills. Medium heroism, then. He laughed.

"I *was* always funny," he said out loud.

Now that it was sort of happening, he wasn't depressed anymore. He was curious. Really curious. Even though he had been brought up to believe that suicide is Your Ticket to Hell, he wasn't afraid of that. Quite simply, he didn't believe in hell. Because he didn't believe in God. In fact, that was a huge part of the problem. He wished he could believe in God. He really wished it. But every time he tried to imagine the truths taught him by his parents and the Bible and a thousand well-meaning people, he couldn't think of them as anything but fairytales. Wishful thinking. It made him very sad.

And unlike a lot of people who found the absence of God to be a relief, it was the thing that made him more lonely than anything. It was The Thing. If he could believe that God knew him, loved him, he could probably bear it, because then he could talk to God about everything, his doubts, triumphs, insecurities, disappointments, loneliness, the inscrutable all of it.

But he couldn't believe in the God, and so he had no one to talk to. For a time, for a long time, he could bear it because he was able to lose himself in the forgetful ecstasy music provided him, and also because he found a few gathering metaphors to describe his inability to believe, his longing to believe. But lately those things had broken down, and he had broken down with them.

The upside was, it made the consequences of suicide easier to bear. What was on the other side of this life? Sweet, perfect nil. Very clean. He could hardly wait.

Okay, how to do this? He looked around for an easy way to get on the rail. It was sturdy enough. A little rounded maybe, but solid. At the corner of the balcony, he found he could leverage himself up onto it, using the wall for balance. Thankfully, he was athletic enough to lift himself in one smooth motion.

"Wow, if my body knew what I was up to, it would kill me," he observed.

So now the moment.

Funny, he thought he would be more emotional. All that beckoned now was an immense relief. He stood full on the rail, facing outward, steadying himself with his hand against the wall. The wind blew through his hair and stung his scalp. Probably a good idea not to look down.

No last words. *Just do it.* He pulled his hand away from the wall.

It happened so quickly he had no time to react.

One of his feet went on one side of the rail and his other foot on the other side. And his nuts came down on the rail with 140 pounds of torso above them.

Even as he couldn't breathe, he thought, this is hilarious. For a moment, he straddled the rail, wheezing. Then, he leaned over and tumble-flopped onto the balcony like a caught fish.

He lay there for a long time, not to reflect, but to wait for his nuts to stop screaming.

Why does everything have to be so goddamned funny? He felt like laughing. Actually, he felt like living. Plus, it would be a pain in the ass for everyone else, cleaning up after him.

He realized he was cold. He stood up and went inside. Minus the throbbing, he was suddenly feeling pretty good.

He got himself a new tumbler from the cupboard. Three ice cubes. Two fingers of scotch. He felt like writing. He knew it was a macabre and unacceptable subject, but he was in a mood not to care. Maybe it wasn't okay to talk about, but you get older and you stop caring what's okay and what's not.

Suddenly, he had a picture in his head of a man going through his life. The man started out fully clothed, and the clothes were made of Other People's Expectations. As he walked along he took things off. His coat, his jacket, his tie. Then his pants and socks and so on until he was in his white underwear, just walking along in his underwear. That was what old age was. People getting old enough to stop caring what everyone else thought. At some point, you let your personality hang out in its underwear.

Only, old age had come to him early. His personality had been walking around in its underwear for a long time. He rattled the ice in his glass. A toast to himself then, and down the hatch.

8. BULL'S-EYE

OVER AN HOUR HAS PASSED, and I am still sitting in my chair, at my table beside my bed. Outside my window and across the street, there is a little green park, and so I distractedly watch people mill about, with dogs or children or by themselves. The inky shadows squirting out from the bottoms of the trees are shrinking, because the sun is still making its way to the top of the sky.

I am worried because I have just written a check out to my roommate for the October rent, and he has taken it and left, and I know there is no money to cover it. I wish I could say I am fixated on the challenge of finding the money. Fixated is not the word. More like I come back between short mental vacations and daydreams to the unpleasant reality that I must do something to help my immediate situation.

Rent. Those people look like beetles with clothes on. That guy has a hat. He's probably bald. Where am I gonna get that money? I could call my dad. Too embarrassing, plus I forgot to call him for his birthday. I could sell something. What could I sell? My guitar amp. Man that thing is loud. I don't like loud music. Do I? How am I gonna cover that check? I wish I was an urban cowboy. Then it would be easy. That was a good movie.

Apart from my big nose, my most distinguishing characteristic is that I have no attention span. My head is like a TV controlled by a baby playing with a remote. Problems and feelings and ambitions pass one after another without order or reason. In such a person there can be no deeply seated anythings. The channel changes too quickly for the plot to develop. Life is lived in half-hour segments, where conflicts arise and resolve in the time it takes to eat a Hot Pocket. Things are easy. Even my rent doesn't matter. Not really. I can put it on my credit card if I absolutely must. I could put my rent for an entire year on my credit card, not make a single payment, file bankruptcy, and in two years apply for a housing loan and still probably slide into the mainstream of the American Dream. In modern life, at least where I live, there are no real consequences.

"Nothing matters anymore," I say out loud. I do this when something registers. If I hear it, then it must have happened, and maybe I'll remember better.

I stand up and walk out into the living room in my black sweats and T-shirt. The blinds are pulled. The room is eerily cast in a dull grey glow, lit by an unwilling light.

I let my eyes move randomly around the room. Yellowed plaster walls from the seven generations of tenants who lived here at a time when it was fashionable to smoke. A faded red couch with wooden legs. Once it was nice, but now it's spattered with vague stains, and half of its cushions are strewn about the floor like stuffed animals in a nursery. On the couch, where one of the cushions should be, is instead a bowl of half-eaten cereal. A dozen tall cans of beer (some crushed, some not) sit at odd angles on the TV, on the windowsill, the floor. Pieces of an unfinished puzzle lay scattered across the coffee table beneath another six-pack of crumpled Miller Lites. Mixed up with the puzzle pieces and the empty cans are crinkled bits of cellophane — the kind that wrap around cigarette boxes — a rolled-up dollar bill, a few handfuls of change, several scratched lottery tickets, styrofoam bowls of some microwavable Asian delicacy, metal forks, a plastic spoon, a lidless salt shaker still full, a bottle of Tabasco tipped over on the floor, and an unopened box containing a blue Snuggie.

Roommate must have cleaned up a little, I think to myself.

Walking through my debris-strewn living room, I kick a red couch cushion at the TV and flip the switch that turns on the lamp lighting the dartboard on the wall. Click. Three darts in the board. One of them stuck squarely in the red bull's-eye, from yesterday.

I am a creature of habit, like most creatures, and my habit is to begin each day with a round of darts. Or more specifically, I stand there and throw them until I hit the red bull's-eye. It has to be the red. I have a rule. Everything else can be going wrong, but if you hit red bulls then you know you are doing something right. It's an act of self-help, a confidence builder. It might take twenty minutes, or five. If I were to keep track over time, I don't think I would notice a steady improvement — just sometimes it goes well and sometimes it doesn't.

While I toss darts, I think a little more about my situation.

The rent is nothing. *20*

The rent will take care of itself. *double 14*

I have two whole days. *18*

Let's look at the big picture here.

Obviously, I'm not where I thought I would be when I started down this road all those years ago. *18 again*

I aimed for one thing and hit another. *17*

But I was aiming. *triple 13*

I still have that.

Okay, so I'm an aimer. Let's start there. *green bulls*

I'm not a shimmering success. *triple 20*

Or a homeowner. *17 again*

Or a husband.

Or rich. *triple 12*

Or very well organized. *green bulls again*

But I never really set out to be those things. *15*

I was looking for something else.

Something that could be called, what? *double 19*

Truth? Cliché. *triple 20 again*

Great art? Well, yes. *12*

Yes, but something more, too.

I want to know what it's all about. *18 again*

At any cost. *11*

It's not enough to have the bits and pieces. It has to be the whole thing. *missed the board*

It's so annoying to put it this way, and even though I don't really know what it means, I think I have spent my life trying to—

God dammit—*triple 18*

I may as well say it, because it's the truth. I'm looking for God. Because I don't know what else life is for. *green bulls*

There was a time when I was younger that I was confident that I would find him or her or it somewhere if I just kept looking. At some point I lost that confidence. I stopped looking. I gave up. I got drunk. *triple 12*

Which is fine if you're the kind of person who can be happy being a doctor or a middle manager or an alcoholic, but for someone who really needs to know, to know for real, abandoning that search meant something catastrophic.

I look around my living room and shout, mostly for dramatic effect: "Man, this place is a catastrophe!" *Pull the darts out of the board.*

This better happen soon. My arm is getting tired.

The truth is that I am lost. *18*

I have been lost for a long time, but I am real good at laughing about it. *20*

But I'm tired of laughing about it.
Something has to change.

Sometimes the outside world and the inside world line up in one cosmic, centerpunched moment. And of course that moment would come when I make some kind of timid resolution to begin once more this near-impossible task of finding my way back to the path I once so boldly strode.

In fear and apprehension, but with the boundless, irrepressible sense of hope that has been the mainstay of my life, I flick the dart across the room and watch it sink deep into the center of the red bull's-eye with a loud *schlock.*

"Great. Now what?"

9. THIS IS PROBABLY A CLUE OF SOME KIND

NOW THEN, LET'S NOT be too hard on ourselves. We've got our little loves, we've got our favorite flavor of soda pop. Even I, in my misguided search for escape and glory, even I have some redeeming qualities.

"Good taste in shoes?" I ask out loud, looking down. Two solid brown oxfords with a square toe and raised heel admire me back. They are hard to focus on, though, because they are attached to feet that are walking. My feet.

I am on my way to the McDonald's, not because I'm terribly hungry but because there is no toilet paper at my house. After throwing my winning dart and vowing to take back the night for God, I had to poop. And because I can't go anywhere without dressing like I'm auditioning for Real World: Willamsburg, a hasty self-adornment ensued.

I pulled on jeans (Paige Laurel Canyon, size 28), a striped yellow-and-brown, snug-fitting shirt with just enough wear as to suggest indifference, a ridiculous bright blue belt with muted silver inlays, and those square, clunky shoes. I left the house twice. The first time I had gotten almost across the street before I realized I forgot my fake glasses.

But now, everything is in place and I can walk down to the McDonald's with my head held high. It's a perfect autumn day, and there's an odor of sweet decay in the air which is very pleasant. I'm walking through the park and there are trees everywhere. All around me gold leaves are dropping from their branches like daredevils, and I think, wow, just like me.

Of all the billions of items and instances in the world — hockey games and glassware and Wall Street and chickens — there is only one sound for each. One unique sound, belonging exclusively and forever to that individual thing. The sound of wooden-soled shoes walking on crisp dried leaves over smooth concrete is the only sound like it in the history of the world. And there it is right now, playing just for me. I want to make a T-shirt that says, "Why are you not constantly astounded?"

Now I make my way along the pond in the center of the park. A dozen geese float on the brown metallic water, facing different directions, honking at each other like siblings. In front of me, two old black men sit on a bench. One of them has a rough full beard frosted with grey and a bright red stocking cap. It looks like he is telling a story, because his hand is raised high over his head to make a point. The other man is laughing, and as I walk past I glance over and see deep creases around the laughing man's eyes and I think, now here is a person well-acquainted with joy.

I pass them, and instinctively, with both hands, I touch the skin around my eyes and make a smiling face. The skin bunches up nicely underneath my fingers. I will make a fine old man. I have always thought so.

Suddenly I return to what I was thinking when I was shooting darts. About God and being lost. I stop walking for a second to collect my thoughts.

Maybe God is a laughing old black man hiding behind fake glasses.

This sounds plausible. I start walking again.

Past the pond now, I see in the distance the sign for the McDonald's. I like this McDonald's because it is fancy. They have a flat-screen TV tuned to CNN. You feel like you are at an airport. Only there are a lot of homeless people in there because it is across the street from the park. So, not quite like an airport.

As I push in the front door, I think about a girl I used to know who came through this same door and cried over her Happy Meal because she saw a one-armed homeless man ask her name.

The bathroom is conveniently located just to my right. I duck in. It is cleaner than my bathroom at home.

Upon exiting I think, well, I'm here. They'll start serving lunch in seven minutes. I have a chance of getting the day's first batch of french fries. I think I'll stick around.

While I wait, I watch the people behind the

counter, and I remember another thing I like about this McDonald's. There is a pretty even balance between black workers and white. It's unusual. It seems like most of the time, around here, every McDonald's is one or the other. But this mix is interesting, like Memphis. Suddenly, I notice it's an Otis Redding song playing through the ceiling speakers.

And then, without warning, the McDonald's turns into a living theater of the modern and weird.

In walks a man with an earring and a blue T-shirt and tinted glasses that obscure his eyes. It looks like he is in his early forties. He has white skin tanned to a workingman's bronze, and his quick movements suggest he is from a place farther north and east than here. Everything about him is boney and sharp: chin, shoulders, nose. He moves up to the counter, and while he waits impatiently for someone to take his order, an older black lady steps up to the register beside him.

Suddenly, he turns to her: "Look, babe. You were just sitting in your car. I would have done it to anyone. It's not a racist thing, even though I know you think it is. Jesus." He turns to the guy behind the counter, who has his hair in cornrows, and says, "McDouble. Large Coke."

The woman looks at him and doesn't say anything. She turns and says her order to the girl at the register. I can't hear what it is.

The man looks behind him. We make eye contact. I don't have time to wonder what it is about me that makes strangers want to confess because he has already turned completely around to face me, saying:

"So I'm driving down West End, and I turn into the parking lot because I got a delivery to make, and Old Black Betty (jerking thumb gesture) pulls out in front of me, and now I can't go anywhere, and we're both stuck in the parking lot, and so I say 'What the fuck lady!' and she just looks at me like I'm a racist! These people!"

He's not quite shouting, but I'm pretty sure he's talking to her, only disguising it as talking to me. The guy in cornrows behind the counter is watching us. I am not happy to be participating in this scene. I want to ask Earring just exactly how someone looks at someone else like they're a racist, but then I remember how at the end of *Stand By Me* the main character makes a voice-over saying how after they all grew up, the other guy in the movie, his best friend, was stabbed to death at a McDonald's trying to break up a fight, and this guy with the sharp cheekbones is real high-strung, and while I am a fan of interesting situations, I don't want things to get too crazy, so I say the first thing I think of, which is:

"I can't decide if I'm gonna get the fish filet meal or just the sandwich."

Otis is still singing, and you can hear the CNN lady on the TV saying something about health care, and the guy in cornrows smiles, and the boney man says, "You're pretty cute, aren't you, princess?" but he turns around and grabs the sack that is waiting for him and jerks his way out the door he came through.

Then the scene is over, and the little black lady turns to me and says, "Get the meal honey," and carries her enormous styrofoam cup over to the place where the ice and soda pop are.

I do what the lady tells me, and while I carry my tray to the table by the window I think, this is probably a clue of some kind.

10. TWITTER TRANSLATOR

I BOUGHT AN APP for my phone yesterday called the "twitter translator." It translates tweets.

I don't really know how it works but it seems like it reduces tweets to their basic meaning. Handy!

I have had it for a day and its probably translated about forty-five messages.

What's weird is that it always boils the message into one of two translations

I'm lonely.

I love you.

Editorial note: I think this story is not a story at all, but I have had enough people tell me they really like it that I find myself in the uncomfortable position of possibly not knowing what I'm talking about. If you guys think it says something people need to hear, then okay, fine. Otherwise, I can live without its inclusion in this collection.

11. PRO WRESTLING

"**YOU'RE NOT EXACTLY A SURE BET**," she was saying, the tips of her fingers delicately grasping a half-eaten spare rib. "For one, your moods swing harder than a wiffle ball bat. For two, the stories you've told me yourself about your past relationships would give any sensible girl pause."

Shay raised the rib back to her mouth and bared her teeth, more than necessary for the task of meat removal. The subtlety was not lost on him.

Simon watched her tear flesh from bone, and then said,"Well, first of all, I take issue with your word choice. *Wiffle* has a dismissive quality. I would like it better if you thought of my moods as swinging more like hickory or aluminum. Something with substance." He put a forkful of collard greens into his mouth.

"Are you saying there's substance to your craziness?"

He took a moment to finish chewing. "Again, word choice. And of course I'm saying that. Before you sits a man well acquainted with rejection, defeat, public humiliation, afflicted with at least four of the seven deadly sins . . ."

"Which four?" she interrupted, her eyes narrowing slightly.

Surprised, Simon thought hard, retrieving his mental archive of, not the Bible, but that one movie with Brad Pitt. "Well, sloth, that's one. I'm pretty lazy. Avarice. I can't remember what that means, but I probably have it . . . then there's the one where the guy had to cut off a pound of his own flesh."

"Greed," Shay said. "It means the same thing as avarice."

"Yeah, greed. But, well, maybe I don't have that one. I mean, maybe I do, but I can think of other more obvious ones."

"So can I." Shay set the finished bone down on the plate. While she drew a fresh napkin from the pile on the table, she said, "Anyway, they're sins, not diseases. It's not a question of either having or not having them. Everyone has them. By degrees."

"How do you know? I thought you were agnostic, right?"

Simon suddenly felt like this was the wrong thing to say, that he had taken the bait. Up to this point, he had been enjoying their playful tête-à-tête, but now it was getting a little too, what was the word? Serious.

Throughout their six-month relationship, Shay had more or less gone along with his conversational preferences, for which there were only two rules: keep it light and wit trumps all. But lately she was starting to do things to steer their pleasant chats toward weightier subjects, into the Here Be Dragons part of his world. He didn't exactly resent her for it, but it made him uncomfortable, and if there was anything he didn't like, it was being uncomfortable.

She didn't immediately reply, so he used the opportunity to make one more attempt to regain the original spirit of the occasion. Levity was everything. He had to try.

Simon held the fork in his hand and pointed the tines at her. "And getting back to your first statement. Nothing is a sure bet, right? I mean, except these collard greens!" This he followed with his winningest smile.

She gave him an unimpressed look and dabbed the napkin at the corner of her mouth. She sat up very straight and in a smooth, deliberate motion set the napkin down and lifted the tumbler of bourbon from its place beside her plate. He heard the cubes of ice jingle against themselves and watched her upper lip swell slightly as it pressed against the wet rim of the glass. Watching him, she took a long, slow sip, swallowed, and returned the glass to the table.

Shay said, "Sometimes I can't tell if I'm dating a charlatan or a chickenshit."

He chose to ignore her tone, even as he realized his happy ship was sailing away without him.

"Charlatan for sure. I mean, I'll sell you a paragraph when a sentence would do, but a coward I am not." He leaned forward dramatically. "Baby, I'll arm wrestle you right now."

He made like to sweep the plates from the table, but he already knew he had blown it. She looked away. After a beat, she leaned over and began to rummage through the purse hanging from the back of her chair. He pretended not to watch.

Then she stopped looking and straightened herself once more. She pushed a bit of runaway hair behind her ears. He decided not to ask her what she was looking for.

Instead, he surveyed their surroundings while he thought of what to do next. The restaurant was not as crowded as he assumed it would be. It was Valentine's Day, after all. Then again, not too many Valentine dates choose to celebrate their love at a roadside BBQ joint in Dickson County. They were only twenty miles outside the city where they lived, but ready examples of modern life in rural America were evident everywhere. Heavy makeup on fat faces, a bloom of backwards baseball caps. He was doing his part, drinking Bud Light from a plastic cup.

He hoped she would say something, but as their hiccup stretched from moment to minute, it was clear he was the one expected to speak first.

Reluctant as Simon was to open an emotionally engaged discussion on any subject, much less the nature of their relationship, it seemed like there was no way out. The keys were in her purse.

He drank off half the beer in one gulp and cleared his throat. "You know, I was married once."

He knew she did not know. He thought that made it a good choice. A little shock value to put her on the back foot.

If Shay was surprised, she didn't show it. He looked at her closely as he spoke, watching for a caught breath or a flinched eye. But she was denying all pleasures.

"I figured," she said. "When?"

"Why figured?"

She shrugged. "There's something about you that's always hiding. Like, you have to keep dancing, or else people will figure out your music stopped. Something's at the bottom of it."

"Wait. Do you think my music stopped?"

"No. God. No one's music ever stops. It's just some people think it's up to the them to make it play, and some people just enjoy the song."

"You are tempting me to marvel at the analogy."

"See, you're dancing right now. You're trying to keep it all going."

Her face had taken on a piercing look he had never seen before. He frowned, thinking of a Saturday morning cartoon he liked when he was a kid. Muppet Babies. You had to get up early to see it. He remembered the episode where the gang—Baby Fozzie, Baby Rolf, Baby Gonzo—they all confronted Baby Miss Piggy because she was being a know-it-all and everyone was sick of it. He had felt bad for Baby Miss Piggy.

He was trying to remember what she said to her Muppet Baby aggressors when he heard Shay's voice.

"Simon, when were you married?" she was saying.

He blinked his eyes. "Oh. Like forever ago. I was a kid. Eighteen."

"I want you to tell me what happened. But first, I want you to get the check so we can go. We're going to be late." She stood up, took her purse from the back of her chair, and walked toward the restroom.

He had almost forgotten. The BBQ wasn't the central panel in this triptych. They were on their way to something else. His childish excitement came back. They were going to a small-time pro-wrestling match at a county fairgrounds in rural Tennessee. He took a deep breath and smiled at no one. The promise of adventure worked a miracle on his spirits. The evening might end well after all.

He paid the check and they walked outside. She seemed to be in a better mood. She handed him the keys from her purse.

"Would you mind driving?"

"Only if you touch my leg intermittently."

Shay didn't say anything, so Simon listened to the sound of their procession across the gravel lot: his steps a slurred speech, hers a crisp, even stitch. That she was an artist on high heels was one thing he liked about her.

Suddenly, she stopped.

"The stars," she said, releasing his arm, looking up.

It was true. The sky was a broken piñata of speckled

infinity. More stars than he had seen in a long time. Simon turned in a circle, taking it in.

He looked for the familiar constellations. He found two of them. Just above the horizon was that most famous constellation, the one that even children recognized. He followed with his eyes the two stars in the front most part of the spoon over to where the handle of its smaller companion began. He looked at the dark place between. He caught a satellite moving in a perfect line of twinkling stealth.

Simon liked to think he had the capacity to articulate the specific nature of whatever phenomena his mind encountered, but the truth was that his talents were no match for the eternal thing which lay before him now. It was almost frightening in a way, the naked night sky. He had nothing to offer but clichés.

They looked on, quiet. A church hymn came to him. *Oh Lord my God when I in awesome wonder, consider all the worlds Thy hands hath made.*

"Do you know that one?" he heard himself say, "'How Great Thou Art?'"

She forgave his non sequitur. "You know I don't know any of them. I didn't go to church." She was facing the other way, looking at different stars.

He felt sorry for her suddenly. Scientific woes aside, the liturgical effort of earnest people through the centuries to artfully describe their relationship to the world around them was one of religion's great gifts to mankind. Lots of beautiful things came out of it. Buildings, stories, the artificial arrangement of stars into shapes that resembled terrestrial items, if only vaguely. However faulty the enterprise, Simon felt like applauding them for making a good try. Profound truths can only be stammered at, after all, or sung about. Or avoided, which was the door he and his friends mostly chose to walk through. Almost everyone he knew — even the smart ones — would rather binge watch a serial TV show than read Dante. And, okay, maybe there's nothing wrong with that. But isn't it good to be occasionally speechless, to shrink back before the sheer magnitude of the universe and feel small, and maybe even holy?

Shit, why was he being so serious all of the sudden? He needed to scale it back.

Simon turned toward her part of the sky, said, "Stars would be a lot more exciting if they'd move around a little, you know? Show some interest. But no, they just lay there, shining like happy dolts."

Hmm, maybe this was overcompensating a little. He read disapproval in her face. He fumbled for some middle ground.

"Look over there," he said, grasping. "Do you see that cluster of stars? The Pleiades."

"No."

"It's really faint, see where I'm pointing?"

She said she did.

"Now look just off to the side. You should be able to see them. For some reason, not looking directly works."

Her smile registered his success. He clocked the win, sufficiently encouraged to continue.

"There used to be some debate, you know, in the olden days, whether the stars in the Pleiades were actually related physically or whether it was just a chance alignment. They thought maybe the stars only appeared to be close to each other when they actually weren't."

"What did they decide?"

"They're related, baby. Locked in a square dance of gravity. There's, like, a thousand stars in the cluster. You can see maybe nine or so with the naked eye."

Still looking at the cluster, she said, "How do you know all this?"

"I spend a lot of time on Wikipedia. Random, unrelated information is the mark of the modern intellectual."

Now she looked at him. "Intellectual is pushing it. Let's go watch some pretend wrestling."

She retook his arm, and they walked the rest of the way to her car, a dark blue Audi coup with a six-speed manual transmission. He opened her door, deciding if they ever broke up he would think of the sixth speed as a perfect illustration of her addiction to control. In the current circumstances, he preferred to view it more as an affinity for precision. Either way, the car was fast and smelled new.

He waited while she lowered herself inside and then eased the door closed behind her.

Making his way around the car to the driver's door, he felt a pang of guilt. He had thrown a friend under the bus in a weak moment. He paused, cleared his throat formally, and addressed the universe.

"I'm sorry I called you guys shiny dolts," he said. "I don't really think that."

TWENTY MINUTES LATER, they arrived at the Dickson County Fairgrounds. Both were in a bad mood.

It was his having been married. No, it wasn't that. It was Simon's refusal to discuss further an event in his past that she felt had obviously left a mark on his present. Just before leaving dinner, he had revealed his marriage, once, a long time ago. He had alluded to it ending badly. It was the first time in their six-month relationship he had acted even slightly vulnerable.

Shay had been waiting for this, for something true — instead of funny or interesting — to fill in the outlines of a personality more prone to parry than reveal. What he had said at dinner showed her he knew he had bruises and could even point at them, describe their color and shape. It was exciting to her. He had married young and divorced. Okay, fine, tell us more.

He could not. During the short drive from the Pleiades to pro wrestling, he reclaimed his former tone of jovial evasion. To each of her questions, he responded with an equanimity calculated to infuriate. How long had they been married? *Long enough to know he didn't like it.* What was she like? *Like a wife, except with fewer opinions.*

Shay watched him as drove. He held the steering wheel firmly in both hands, his eyes moving from the road to the speedometer to the gas gauge to her eyes and back to the road. She slid her tongue between the molars and bit down until she tasted blood.

While her displeasure was rooted in her frustration at his inability to participate in a conversation of any depth whatsoever, his was due to his being asked in the first place. After all, he felt, he had only told her because he wanted to shock her. To him, it was just another amusing thing to say. Instead of shock, she interpreted the announcement as an invitation to explore the backrooms of his personality, which, frankly, was rude. He finally told her as much, in a tone slightly harsher than he intended, and she responded to his comment by not responding, to that or anything else he said after. The silent treatment. Very grown up. He said that, too. She looked out the window. He fumed. The car performed flawlessly.

By the time they rolled into the second gravel parking lot of the night, a thin frost was accumulating on the windshield from the inside. He cut the power and removed himself. She followed.

They walked at arm's length through a full parking lot surrounded by a tall chain-link fence. They were in the space farthest from the door, so he had plenty of time to walk and be angry. Her steps sounded more arrogant than poised, he decided.

The building they approached was a gymnasium-sized box of stacked white cinder blocks, made yellow under a single buzzing streetlamp. No windows, but a four-on-the-floor beat pressed its lower frequencies through a double door of curtained glass. A man with long, curly, oiled black hair stood to the right of the door, watching a small dog pee into the dirt at the end of a nylon leash. He did not look up as they passed.

The double door was the only way forward. Simon grabbed the left handle and pulled. Locked. He moved to the right handle and pulled again and the door swung open.

"I hate it when they do that," he said, holding wide the door for her. Shay did not look at him as she went inside.

"SUUUUUPER HUUUUUUNNNK!"

The sound was incredibly loud.

Simon blinked his eyes against the enveloping white light and tried to understand what was happening.

What was happening was a man with a pinched, sweaty forehead was shouting into a small handheld microphone. He was standing just inside the door Simon and Shay had come through, so they were right on him, beside him. Flecks of spittle hung in the air like mist. His round, heavy body trembled beneath a red satin windbreaker embroidered with some words in cursive about a trucking company. There was no hair on the head, no shame in the delivery, only an incredibly loud homage to masculine beauty spraying from mouth to mic.

The object of his invocation stood in the center of the room, standing alone, quiet, reverent, like Macbeth in the third act, except mostly naked. His tanned and oiled body was covered only by knee-high boots and a black speedo. While Simon and Shay watched, the man called Super Hunk dramatically bowed his head, apparently praying for strength in the great battle before him.

Satin Jacket finished yelling Super Hunk's name, and a distinct moment of silence flushed the room. Simon looked at Shay, who seemed to be transfixed by the drama. Into her ear he whispered, "I think I've seen that guy at the Y."

Shay's face started to smile, but was jolted into a flinch as a tidal wave of '80s dance-pop broke through the room. *I'm Too Sexy.*

At this, Super Hunk threw his head up, toward God and the gym lights, and spread his arms wide, inviting the crowd to worship his moderately developed musculature. The spotty crowd responded with an applause made inaudible in the crashing music.

Simon was fully invested in the spectacle when he felt a sharp tug on his coat. He turned to see another bald-headed man trying to get his attention. This man was much smaller than Satin Jacket, and older, seated at a fold-up table beside the door. A small metal box and a spool of red ticket stubs lay before him on the table. Oh yes. Admission. Nine dollars or ten dollars, the sign said. The old man was saying something Simon couldn't understand about difference in price, and why. "I'M TOO SEXY FOR MY SHIRT, TOO SEXY FOR MY SHIRT," was the only sound in the room.

Suddenly the voice was back. "ARE YOU STUDENTS?" came bellowing over the PA. The beat throbbed on, unmolested. Simon looked and realized the man in the satin windbreaker was talking to them. He was trying to help sort out the confusion, but through either forgetfulness or a relentless dedication to being heard, he was talking to Simon through the mic.

"IT'S NINE DOLLARS FOR STUDENTS, TEN FOR ADULTS. KEITH, YEAH, GO AHEAD AND DO NINE FOR THEM. THEY SEEM LIKE NICE PEOPLE."

Simon handed him a twenty and said, "It's okay. Keep it."

The man named Keith counted out two one-dollar bills and handed them over anyway. Simon took them and turned to leave.

"KEITH, STAMP THEIR HANDS."

Simon turned back toward the table and put his hand out and Shay put her hand out and Keith reached out with a trembling hand of his own and made swift work with a larger-than-necessary rubber stamp. Blue ink. "BBQ."

Shay looked at her hand with the wonder of a child. "They like the same things we do!" she said.

While they made their way to their seats, the man

called Super Hunk was doing his Final Countdown routine. Arms in various positions of excellence: the classic muscleman, the shoot-for-the-sky, the one where pecs are flexed to the beat of the music.

"I like that one," Shay said, nodding her head in the direction of the ring. She seemed to be getting into it.

The Too Sexy music played well into the second chorus while Super Hunk flexed at people. Then a strange thing happened. He extended one of his arms through the ropes, where a very large woman with grey permed hair and not a few wrinkles greedily seized it in both hands. She bent over her prize, and Simon and Shay gasped as a tiny pink tongue poked out of the mouth and licked the top of the wrestler's hand in what could only be described as an act of lust. The wrestler did not withdraw his hand, nor did anyone in the audience make any special fuss. The lick lingered for a few seconds when a skinny pale man — either an usher or her husband — gently took her arm and led her back to her seat. Super Hunk rose from his knees and pointed at his admirer with an expression that said, "I'm doing this for you, baby."

Simon was delighted. He turned to Shay. "It's like reverse chivalry with a bawdy twist! I'm getting nachos!"

He stood up from his seat and walked over to the improvised concessions, which consisted of another folding church-style table with several paper boats of tortilla chips arranged next to a crock pot of what Simon assumed was melted Velveeta. CANDY ALSO AVAILABLE read a sign.

Simon received his nacho boat and stood for a moment to examine his surroundings more closely.

The ceiling cast a bright white light down onto a crowd of about fifty people, in a room that could hold four hundred. They were mostly white and mostly fat, evenly arranged in pockets of twos and threes around the four sides of the ring in folding chairs that did not extend more than three rows deep. Sweatpants were prominent. Simon saw a kid who could not have been older than fourteen roll up his sleeve to reveal to his friend a shoulder tattoo. It was a skull with balls of fire where its eyes would be. The friend extended a pointer finger to touch it, but the one with the tattoo punched him hard on the shoulder. A lone heavyset black woman with hair peroxided orange stood up, moved two seats over and sat down again.

By now, the music had stopped, and another man had quietly appeared to act as Super Hunk's adversary. Simon return to his place beside Shay to report his findings.

"This is *actual America*," he said.

Shay withdrew a chip from the boat. "The other one didn't get any theme music or poses," she said.

Simon looked. Super Hunk was no longer alone in the ring. He was being circled by a heavy man in a bright green sleeveless spandex onesie.

"Who's that guy?" Simon asked.

"That's Turtleman," came a voice from behind. "He sucks."

Simon turned to see the black woman with the orange hair. She had moved again.

"You keep moving," Simon observed.

"Can't get comfortable," she said. "Something wrong with these chairs. Like they might got a disease or something."

"What kind of disease?" Simon asked.

"Nacho cheese disease! Whooo hooo!!" exclaimed the woman, slapping her thigh and standing up. Suddenly, she was serious, eyeing Simon over her shoulder with suspicion while she moved a few seats over and sat down.

Simon turned back around.

"That lady should wrestle," he said.

Meanwhile, Turtleman kept circling the Hunk, who in turn kept turning to face him. Turtleman's thinning hair was dyed green, except that was maybe a month ago and now it was mostly grey. He looked twenty years older than Super Hunk. He had heavy bags under his eyes and an overripe body that resembled, well, a turtle.

"Turtleman doesn't look so healthy," said Shay.

While Simon and Shay watched, a very small Hispanic man in a referee shirt and a perfect flattop slid under the ropes and into the ring. He stood up in the center and gestured that the wrestlers should join him there. He said something inaudible to each of them, and the bell sounded.

The men immediately locked arms.

"Beat his green ass!" That was the voice of the lady with the pink tongue.

Hunk's opening move was to stomp on Turtleman's foot. It missed by six inches, but Turtleman grimaced obediently and the crowd cheered.

"Amazing," Simon said.

Next, Hunk put Turtleman into some kind of standing headlock. The source of the victim's pain was unclear, but he kept waving his arm frantically, pathetically, making gasping sounds.

"He's choking!" called out a young girl with glitter on her face.

Suddenly, the situation was reversed. Now, it was Turtleman doing the choking. His laugh was maniacal.

"Take that, you little bitch!" he yelled.

"Jesus, there's kids here," Simon said to Shay, who responded by grabbing his hand.

"I'm not sure I like this," she said.

Suddenly, the situation was reversed again. Super Hunk had implausibly lifted Turtleman high above his head. He fell backward onto the mat, and the Turtleman landed with a loud crash.

The crowd went crazy. The boy with the skull tattoo raised his fist, shouted, "Fuck yeah!"

Super Hunk leapt up and raised wide his arms. He pointed at Pink Tongue. Turtleman remained on the floor. Something about the way he moved seemed off. Like the acting was on pause.

To Simon's surprise, Super Hunk bent down,

took Turtleman's arm, and pushed him through the ropes and onto the concrete floor directly in front of Simon and Shay. The ousted wrestler raised his arms to break the fall, but he wasn't moving more than necessary. Simon and Shay had to scoot back their chairs to avoid being part of the action. Turtleman lay at Simon's feet, breathing heavily. A rank odor of sweat and alcohol.

Super Hunk lowered himself through the ropes and grabbed a handful of Turtleman's grey-green hair. Turtleman rose to his feet.

Super Hunk drove Turtleman's face into the corner of the mat. It didn't look fake.

Simon glanced at Shay, whose face was the picture of alarm.

Turtleman sank to his knees. Super Hunk punched him in the back of the head. Definite contact.

Simon looked at the referee, whose eyes reflected that something was wrong. The whole scene was playing out right in front of them. Simon could see the cigarette stains in Super Hunk's teeth when he smiled. From his place inside the ring, the referee was yelling, "Jeff, what the fuck are you doing?"

The other man didn't answer. He grabbed Turtleman by the spandex and tried to push him into the ring. The spandex split open and the man's back fat pressed through the hole, ungainly and pale. The crowd jeered. Simon looked around. No one seemed to sense that this person was in danger. A hostile energy permeated the room, the crowd coalescing into a mob. Eyes narrowed to slits. Everyone yelling. Children watching with mouths open. Pink Tongue was at the side of the ring with her hands on the ropes, hurling insults.

Turtleman slowly climbed the rest of the way into the ring and tried to get to his knees. Blood was pouring from his nose in a thick rivulet, rapidly spreading through the green spandex in a wide black stain. His expression was vacant.

The referee waved that the fight was over.

When you see a violent act committed up close, it sears itself in your mind like a hot iron. Your awareness, sensing the gravity of the situation, sharpens your senses to needles, inscribing the event on your memory like a tattoo. For the rest of your life and at odd intervals—at a pet's funeral, in line at the grocery store—you will suddenly recall the exact color of the lost blood, the sound of the mobbing crowd, the tangy smell of the melted cheese, the pressure of her hand in yours as you both become unwilling witnesses to one person causing serious harm to another.

Super Hunk climbed back into the ring and swaggered toward Turtleman, who was bent over on hands and knees. Hunk said something Simon couldn't hear, and then he spit on the back of the man's head. It was crawling off the neck in a slow ooze when Super Hunk swung back his booted leg in a dramatic arc and brought it around full force into the downed man's face. Turtleman's head snapped back and fell forward with his body onto the floor. The sound it made was the thing Simon would remember most. It wasn't like the movies.

The man in the satin jacket was now inside the ring, pulling Super Hunk away while the referee crouched beside the unconscious wrestler. Blood was pooling around the man's head.

"Please, let's go," said Shay quietly. Tears rimmed her eyes.

Simon squeezed her hand. "Do you think we should call 911?"

Shay didn't answer. They rose and hastened through the crowd, the members of which were no longer cheering. The kid with the tattoo looked like he was about to cry. Simon felt a little glad about that.

There was a police car in the parking lot with a policeman inside it. Simon approached the car and the policeman rolled his window down. Simon continued to hold Shay's hand while he explained what he'd seen. The policeman responded that an ambulance was already on its way.

"Shouldn't you go arrest that guy in the boots?" Simon asked.

The policeman said they were looking into it.

"It seems pretty clear a man was assaulted."

"Yeah, but it's wrestling," said the cop. "People get hurt."

12. HOQUIAM

LAST NIGHT, OUT IN HOQUIAM, Washington, the moon rose all flat and round like a big white plate. I come here sometimes to help my friend Sarie restore an old house she bought. Sarie is sixty-eight, and the house is over a hundred, but she is giving it a new birthday. On weekends, she drives down from Bellingham in her Prius to install new wiring, sand the hardwood floors, tear down the rotten chimney. Sometimes I am with her but most times not.

Look at Sar: a little bird-shaped woman with honey-brown hair and fine wrinkles around her mouth, she moves like a movie in fast forward. Darting into the kitchen to grab a crowbar, then down on her hands and knees in the bathroom to scrape off the old linoleum.

I've been here three nights of the five I'll spend, and I have to tell you about the conversation I had yesterday evening at Stuffy's, the bar we go to after work. Stuffy's has a strange name and free wi-fi and a dozen microbrews on tap, so it would be my favorite place to go even if it weren't in a backwoods town out in the wet corner of ancient America.

One night, this happens:

Sarie and I drive over to Stuffy's for hot wings and coleslaw. She brings her own wine in a plastic Odwalla container and asks the bartender for a glass of water. She promptly drinks the water and fills the glass up with wine. I order the local IPA.

We eat and talk about how cheap the shower door is at the Home Depot versus the local place, who's likely to win the democratic nomination, my girl trouble, her girl trouble, and then she's done with the wine and the coleslaw, and so she takes the car home. I hang out to email and watch ultimate fighting on the high def.

While I'm sitting there, the guy who cooked my hot wings comes out from the kitchen and sits down almost next to me at the bar, a seat between us. He is sort of fat, thirtyish but with grey hair and thin glasses that make him look smart. He still has his apron on and is already half done with his glass of beer.

We watch two men beat the spit out of each other on the TV, and we both shout when one of them lands a nasty punch. He looks over at me and lifts his beer, in a "cheers-to-that" sort of way. I nod knowingly.

During the commercial break, he asks me how did I like my hot wings. So I tell him the truth, which is that they were pretty good but not very hot.

He says, "Yeah, I'd like 'em to be hotter, but that's

how they come out of the freezer, so that's the way I cook 'em."

He asks me where I'm from so I tell him the short story, Tennessee. He says, "Where else?" so I say I went to school in Bellingham but moved down to Seattle in '03 and then Nashville a few years ago, and I've come back to play a show in Seattle and in the meantime am helping my mom work on her house. Sarie is not really my mom but everything else is true.

He doesn't say anything to that so I ask him where he's from.

He says, "Here. Except I was away for a few years, and then I came back."

I say, "Oh yeah, where'd you go?"

"Shelton."

Just then, the TV fight comes back from commercial, and we both turn and sip beer. While we watch I think about what he just said. The way he said it. And I realize that Shelton didn't mean Shelton the town thirty miles away, it meant Shelton the medium-security prison next to the town.

I want to ask him about it, but the fight is on. Ah, but I am in luck, because less than two minutes into it, the one in the white trunks has pinned the one in black and is hitting him repeatedly in the face with his elbows, and so the referee stops the fight.

My friend with the apron and the wire-rimmed glasses slaps his hand down on the bar in triumph and takes a long gulp from his beer. I wait a moment, and then I say, "Hey, what did you do?"

He looks at me blankly. I look back and wait.

"When?"

I say, "Shelton."

He turns and watches the TV through the thin glasses, and I can see that I guessed right. I think he is deciding whether or not I'm in the club. But I already know I am.

He picks up the remote from the bar counter and flicks it to mute.

"Have you ever gotten bad news?" he asks.

I don't say anything.

He says, "Well, I got some bad news a few years ago. My mom got killed by a drunk driver."

"That's awful," I say. "I'm sorry."

He says, "Yeah, but the fucked-up part was that the drunk driver was my stepbrother. He was on his way home from a Super Bowl party—this was like 6 years ago—and he ran a red light and clipped my mom's Corolla and knocked it into a telephone pole. It happened just around the corner over there, on Wishkah."

"Wow."

"Yeah," he says, looking at the TV commercial. "Fucked up."

I look at the TV with him, waiting. He takes a sip and says, "Anyway, the dude was an asshole. Before this happened, I mean. The kind of guy who'd beat his own dog if he felt like it. I hated him before my mom married his dad. I hated him the whole time they were married. Still hate him now. I was at work when it happened. My sister called me and told me. She said the stepbrother didn't get hurt at all, that he was in the jail in Aberdeen. Well, I went to the bank and got enough cash to post his bail. Then I went to the jail and got him. And instead of driving home I drove out to the beach in Ocean Shores."

"Yeah?"

"Yeah. You know how you can drive all up and down right on the sand? Well, I drove about six miles past the state park and then I stopped the car and told him to get out. I think he thought I was just gonna leave out there. But I didn't. I beat the living shit out of him right there on the beach. Then I drove back home to Hoquiam."

"Holy shit," is what I say. He doesn't really look like the kind of person who would do that. "Did he fight back?"

"He tried, but he was a little fucker and I'm not. Anyway, I left him there on the beach, bleeding in the sand, and I guess he was there all night until a jogger found him the next morning. They took him to the same hospital my mom died in. Later that day was when they arrested me."

"Wow. How long were you in Shelton for?"

"Two years. It was supposed to be four, but I got out early on good behavior." He looks over at me. "You know, I'm really not that kind. The kind who beats people up. It just had to happen. I'd probably do it again, all things considered."

"What happened to the stepbrother?"

"He's still here, works over at the Home Depot. Got a funny-shaped nose now, but he's still the same asshole, from what I hear." He fingers the foam on the lid of his beer. "People don't change, buddy."

For a second, I watch the reflection of the TV in his glasses. The fight is still on. A new match, new fighters.

Suddenly, he stands up, taps his knuckles on the bar top. "Anyway, gotta get back to the wings. Tell the folks hi in Tennessee."

I start to stand up to shake his hand goodbye, but he is already walking back to the kitchen.

13. BUS STOP

IN NASHVILLE, THE intersection of 12th Avenue South and Wedgewood is what you would call sketchy. Two of the four corners are home to the barred window variety of gas station. A third marks the boundary of a large housing project. And on the last corner sits a covered bus stop—a little bench surrounded on three sides by plexiglass—a favored nightly gathering spot for the surrounding community.

On this particular night, I was putting up posters for a show I had coming up. I am thorough in my postering—partly because it helps get the word out, partly because it is a kind of sanctioned vandalism. Not quite okay, but you won't get arrested for it.

Twelfth and Wedgewood is also one of the most traveled intersections in Nashville—Twelfth being a favorite corridor for the padded white warrior making the daily pilgrimage from Forest Hills to his office job downtown or on Music Row. In the course of a week, half of Davidson County drives through that intersection. So of course I would be there late on a Sunday night with my staple gun and stack of posters. I have a job to do, after all.

What happened was this: my friend Dylan wheeled his silver Honda into the parking lot of the better of the two gas stations to wait while I littered the intersection with advertisements. I jumped out and peppered the nearest pole with staples and paper, and, with an almost subconscious paranoia, kept an eye on the bus stop bench. There were four men sitting side by side, watching me.

As soon as I finished stapling, I looked around and realized the other poles were made of metal and that I would be needing the tape I had left in the car. I started back toward the Honda when one of the men shouted something I couldn't hear. Not to be put off, I turned and shouted back, "I'm sorry?" which is my way of saying, "What did you say?" The man repeated himself. I still couldn't understand, so I had to decide: continue back toward the car, or walk over and hear the man out.

I do like a good adventure.

I jogged across the street to where they were sitting like a panel of judges. They watched me in silence as I came toward them. Drawing near, I could see they were older—two of them were bald, and one of the bald ones was dressed in a blinding white linen tunic and pants, complete with polished white shoes. He was the one who had spoken earlier, I guessed, because when he spoke now, it was the same voice as before.

"Man, what you doin', tackin' your sign all over our telephone poles?"

I couldn't tell what kind of serious he was being, so I answered him straight.

"Dude, I got a show comin up, and I got to let the people know!"

Now one of his friends spoke up. "You mean, like, a music show?"

"Yeah, exactly!" I held one of the posters up and pointed at my name. "That's me."

"You puttin' up posters for your own show?" asked White Shoes, incredulous.

It hadn't really struck me that this was a thing unbecoming of an artist. I thought about it and said: "Man, you got to shout out your own name loud as you can. No one else is gonna do it for you."

"I hear that," said White Shoes, raising his arm to high five me. I met his hand right there. Felt good. White Shoes stood and announced he was going to help me put my posters up. Nothing could have pleased me more. I ran back to the car to get the tape, opening the door to Arcade Fire and a visibly agitated Dylan asking me if I was okay.

"Dude, that guy's gonna help me put up my posters. It's gonna be awesome!" I said. Dylan shot me a worried look and turned up the music.

I ran back to the bench and explained to White Shoes how this was going to go. By way of demonstration, I peeled off four strips of the blue painter's tape I was holding and stuck them on his fingers, one to each. Then, I said he would be the tape peeler and I would place the poster on the pole and we would then peel the pieces of tape off his fingers and onto the paper. He seemed to be fine with that.

It took about fifteen minutes to put twenty posters up on four poles, so we had time to get acquainted.

"So, what are y'all doin'?" I asked. "Just sitting there? I mean, I'm curious."

White Shoes was putting tape on his fingers. "Man, we sit there every Sunday night. Have for years. Sometimes we have a little sip, but tonight we just sittin'. Watching the world go by, you know?"

"Yeah, man, I do that all the time."

He held out his hand to present the tape. For some reason, he put the blue strips of tape on the tops of his fingers instead of the inside like I would. Dark brown fingers with little childish strips of bright blue. I took the first piece and reached up to begin taping one of the corners down.

"Where do you live?" I asked.

He pointed past my head to the housing project. "In there, about four rows back," he smiled. "Been there about thirty-five years."

I took the next piece of tape off his finger. "Thirty-five years is a long time, man. Were you born here?"

"No, I was born in A'lanta. Come up to Nashville after Viet Nam to be with my brother."

"Wait, what? How old are you? Viet Nam was, like, three wars ago."

"I'm fifty-nine years old, pup." He handed me a piece of tape. "But I'm still chasing the ladies like I was eighteen!" He smiled and let out a wheezy little laugh. He had wrinkles around his mouth that made him look sad, and his eyes were yellowish. That was age. But there was still something youthful in him. His skin was smooth, and his teeth were all there and still white.

"I bet you do all right with the ladies," I said.

What he said next I repeat to you only because if I left it out, this story would not be true.

"Man, you don't know *what* goes down over here. People get *crazy*. Let me just say, when you got your fingers in two girls and your dick in a third, then you *know* you partyin'!"

I was glad he didn't reach up to high five me, because my shock was sufficient to make motor function momentarily impossible.

After a beat, I reached for another strip of tape. "Wow. That's, um, pretty crazy. So, like, what do you do for work?"

He was busying his fingers with a new round of blue tape. "I'm an orderly at Belton Tower."

"What's an orderly? Like a nurse?"

He stopped fiddling with the tape and looked at me. "Kid, you don't know anything. An orderly is the one who changes the bed pans and sheets and diapers for the people when they're dyin'."

I will say I was impressed with White Shoes' frankness.

"Oh! How long have you worked there?"

"Man, a long time. Long enough to see some sad shit."

I didn't say anything. I stuck another piece of tape to the corner of the poster. That pole done, we both walked the crosswalk across Twelfth to the next corner, in front of the headlights of the waiting cars. I looked over and saw Dylan sitting in his idling Honda, watching us.

I wanted White Shoes to tell me more about his job, but I didn't want to ask, or didn't know how. But a lot of times, if you want someone to tell you something, all you have to do is not talk, and they will.

We gathered around the telephone pole. I took a piece of tape from his finger and put it up. We were quiet for three strips. Finally, he said: "It's funny. People there. You know that place? Belton Tower. It's where people go when they're at the very end. It's a pretty nice place—it costs a lot of money—so only rich people go there. But they go there to die. And they know it. And their family knows it. And sometimes it takes a long time."

Something in his voice made me pause. An old hustler can turn prophet in the time it takes a light to change from green to red.

He continued: "Man, you know what's weird? These lawyers and bankers and whatever, they have these cars and wives and houses on the beach, and then here they are, just fadin' away. I can't tell you how many times I've been the last person they know in this world."

We both looked up to watch an absolutely gorgeous black Mercedes speed past us.

"What do you mean?"

"I mean people stop coming. You know. The families. Or they come once or twice a week, and they can't wait to get out of there, soon as they come in. But brother, I'm in there every day, day after day, doin' the most personal shit to these people. People who fancied themselves princes, you know? I get to know 'em, and I'm there for 'em, and they know it. They trust me. Man, it'll tear you up."

I thought about that while I did the thing with the tape. Trying to think of something to say. Finally, I said, "That's cool. That it's you. They didn't know it was gonna turn out like that, but here it is, and you're the one who's there. It's you."

I'm not sure White Shoes heard that part, because his yellow eyes glassed over, and I could see him back there in his head, four rows back, thinking of someone I had never met.

"The thing about that job," he said quietly, "is those people pay a lot of money for bein' in there. Sad as it is, there are a lot worse places you could end up. But these orderlies I work with, man, some of 'em, they don't give a shit. They lazy, you know? And I get it. This work is *nasty*. Who wants to clean the shit off some old man's ass? Not me! But that's our job. And these people, some of them, they so sick they can't speak for themselves. They just lyin' up in that bed, day after day, and they can't talk no more. They can't *defend* themselves. And so some of those people I work with, they don't do nothin'. They just let 'em sit there, sometimes for two, three days, in whatever. And that ain't *right*. Man, these old people — I don't care who you are — they deserve some *dignity.* You can't just let a person lay there like that."

White Shoes' glassy eyes were fixed on me now.

"Man, I got my sins, Lord knows. But brother, *I give a shit.* People deserve a little respect. I know people who don't got nothin', never had nothin'. But they still children of God. They still laugh and cry. I know some of the people I take care of are the same ones who drove through this very intersection, lookin' at me like I'm what's wrong with the world. Funny. Then a few years later they all wastin' away, grabbin' my hand, pleading with me in they eyes not to leave the room 'cause they so scared they won't be there to see me come back. Gives you a little, you know, *perspective.*"

We were standing there in front of the gas station with the barred windows, and all the noise in the world was swirling around us. A few blocks away, I could see the lit-up windows of Belton Tower, and I thought how, at that very moment, some old man was lying in his bed thumbing through the pages of his life, afraid.

"Anyway," said White Shoes, "let's finish this up. I got to get back to my friends."

We did the last pole expertly because we had been practicing for three corners. He walked me across the street and back to Dylan's idling car. We stood for a second, awkwardly.

"You should come by the Tower sometime and play for those people. They would love it."

"I'll do it, man. Hey, what's your name?"

He laughed. "It don't matter, pup. I'll be seeing you." He turned and walked across the street toward the bus stop. I stood beside the closed car door and watched him. Halfway across, he turned around and walked back.

"My name's Robert. Can I have five bucks?"

My turn to laugh. I fished some bills out of my pocket. Who wouldn't help out a friend?

14. SUGAR CHEST

I GOT A NEW BIKE. New to me. It cost forty dollars. It has two baskets—one on the handlebars and one behind the seat. And a coaster brake that doesn't really work. Sometimes you have to pedal four times around before it engages. This adds an element of excitement to the biking process.

Last night, I was riding around Nashville, late. It had just rained, so the air was fresh-smelling and cool and the streets were shiny and wet and empty. I was in good spirits. I was riding to my friend David's house to do some last-second tweaks on a new song. On the downhill parts I would put my feet up on the handlebars and roll as far and as fast as I could. On the uphills I would stand and pedal because it's easier, especially when you only have one gear.

I waved to the cop car parked in the lot at Katy Kay's Ranch Dressing. There were two cops in the car—one waved back. Probably, cops have nothing to do on cool summer nights after a rainstorm because everyone's in a good mood and mischief is at a minimum.

As I was cruising down 12th Avenue, I looked down into my front basket. In the basket was a foam rubber case, and inside the case was a hard drive, and inside the hard drive was all the new music I'd been working on for the last month. I looked down at the case while I was riding and thought of something.

A few months ago, I visited the Hermitage, which is the house where President Andrew Jackson used to live. It's just outside Nashville. You can walk through his house and these people meet you in each room and tell you about the high-backed chairs or the French wallpaper or the bells that were connected by wires all throughout the rooms.

I was there with my parents. We walked through the house, and when we got to the kitchen, we found a tall, thin table with a deep drawer and a key lock on the front. The table top was ornately carved and had different colors of wood arranged in a symmetrical pattern. It looked expensive and out of place in the simple kitchen.

Then the lady explained it was a sugar chest. A long time ago, sugar was so precious that people would lock it up in fancy storage boxes. In the days before steamboats, it took forever for a shipment of sugar to come up to Tennessee from New Orleans on a riverboat, and so of course it was very expensive. Because it was so valuable, wealthy families would buy elaborate storage chests of walnut and cherry wood to store their sugar. It was a point of pride for families to own a sugar chest.

It was probably the flat-screen fifty-inch of its day.

So there I was, on my bike, riding over to my engineer's house at one in the morning with my hard drive in the front basket, and I was looking at the soft grey case with the red printed flower. Thinking of the sugar inside it. All the hours and frustration and hope turned into ones and zeros in the modern tradition. But really and still, it was this one person's life—mine—recorded in sound for better or worse, for now and always. My sugar. I was glad I had spent extra on the slightly fancier case. It looked good. It should look good.

That took way longer to write than to think. I was just riding and looking down and thinking of sugar chests and music, and the whole thing took about four seconds. But it was long enough to be distracted, because when I looked up there was a person standing in front of me. For a split second, I thought what, in the hell is that guy doing there I'm going to hit him. And then I realized I was riding on the sidewalk and that's where people walk and so it made sense. But none of that mattered now, because unless I took immediate action, there was going to be a collision between man and bicycle and a very awkward conversation afterward.

I went to brake, but oh yeah, the coaster brake doesn't work that well. After two revolutions backpedaling and still no braking, there was nothing for me to do but swerve hard to the right, which meant careening off the sidewalk and into someone's yard. I picked the wrong yard.

The sidewalk intruder lunged to his right, me to my right. We missed each other but now I had a new set of problems, because apparently this particular homeowner had a thing for large rocks. I'd never really seen this before, but there were these huge river-rock-type boulders placed randomly in the yard. I missed the first one, but the second caught my front wheel rudely, and at this point, I knew it wasn't going to end well.

I fought to keep my balance, but then there appeared directly in front of me a kind of offset wall of mortared rock that rose two feet. I had just enough time to think, God, I'm too old for this.

The front wheel plowed squarely into the wall, and, for only the second time in my life, I went over the handlebars. I couldn't see what I was going to land, on because the trees on the far side of the yard made the shadows oblique. I heard the bike clatter against the rocks behind me, and I heard the dude on the sidewalk say, "Dude!" And then suddenly I was on my back, sliding across the grass.

I slid to a stop and lay there for just a second to see if there was any screaming pain. There wasn't. I sat up and looked back toward the sidewalk, and the man I had almost hit was looking at me. He asked if I was alright. I said I was.

I said, "Sorry for almost hitting you. I was daydreaming."

He said, "It's the middle of the night. But okay."

I stood up and still no pain, so I walked back and picked up the bike. The wheel wasn't visibly bent, so I gave it a spin and everything seemed okay. I walked it to the sidewalk, hopped on and gave it little pedal. Nothing wrong there, either. Well, sweet.

Only then did I notice the empty basket. I caught my breath. I thought six things in one second, but the loudest thing was, *I don't have the current song backed up*. Oh shit oh shit oh shit.

I walked back over to the wall, and there was the hard drive, laying in a puddle on the walkway. Well, sweet.

I picked it up carefully. The case was wet. I said out loud with my eyes closed, "To the gods of sugar chests and music, let this be dry inside. Please."

I took a deep breath and unzipped the case. Not dry. Not too wet though, either. I guessed I wasn't going to know until I plugged everything in.

I took the hard drive out. No dents, so I put the wet case back in the basket, tucked the hard drive under my arm, and wished my accidental conspirator well. The air still cool, the street still shiny, I rode the last mile to my engineer's house to see if my sugar was still there.

15. EVERYONE HAS A MIRANDA MOMENT

MAYBE IT'S BECAUSE I'M single again, maybe it's because I'm getting older, maybe it's because my preacher grandpa is wasting away in a Oregon nursing home, maybe it's because my dad had to go to the hospital last week for weird symptoms associated with stroke, but I'm going to write this story down.

I'm writing it because I wish I could pray, and I can't. Somewhere along the way, I stopped believing in it. But maybe this will help.

It's six or seven years ago. I'm living in Seattle, seeing this girl. Miranda. She lives in a place called Ellensburg, a flat little farm town on the other side of the Cascade Mountains. Miranda is what you would call smoking hot. Also, smart, extremely opinionated, and a little bit mean. The kind of girl I like. Well, one of the kinds.

It is late one summer night, we are talking on the phone, and suddenly I get it into my head that I am going to drive to Ellensburg right then. It will take three hours;

I will be there by two. It'll be fun, I say. She doesn't disagree. Spontaneity has always been my co-pilot.

I don't remember much about the drive except the stars were very bright once I got away from Seattle. And the night was so mild I drove with my windows down and went long distances with my head sticking out, looking up. The freeway was empty and very dark.

I pull up to Miranda's house just after two. She is standing on the porch, waiting for me in a black dress and high heels and a smirk. She is always overdressed.

Her slight Spanish accent breezes down from the porch to the front yard. "I can't believe I'm letting you see my house. It looks like a crazy lady lives here."

"It just looks like a house."

"No, the inside, *pendejo*."

We kiss hello, and I follow her through the front door. She is right. It looks like a crazy person lives here. As if she had gone to Goodwill, bought one of everything, and threw each through the front door without looking. There are mattresses leaning up against walls, two bulky TVs (one cracked), faded Mexican blankets covering the windows. A single picture above the couch—a Dali print like a college student would have—hangs crookedly from a bent nail. The table lamp sitting on the floor (no lampshade) casts light upward into our eyes and stretches the shadows behind us, long and creepy.

"Are you sure you're not into meth?" is the obvious question.

She scowls. "If you don't like it, you can leave. I don't have time to clean. It interferes with my reading. Besides, it is an honest reflection of how I feel inside."

"In complete disarray and without any focus whatsoever?"

This time, she looks hurt. "I didn't invite you. You elected to come."

"You could have stopped me."

"Could I have?" She fixes me with hostile smoldering in her almond-brown eyes. "That's what I thought. Now. Sit there on the sofa, *bobo*. Would you like a splash of bourbon?"

Twenty minutes later, the bourbon is gone and the high heels are off and strong are the forces of ecstasy at play. In my whiskey-kissed frolicking, I kick over the shadeless lamp. There is a sound of imploding glass, and the room goes dark.

It is precisely at this moment that my phone rings.

A queer digital light leaps up from the floor and turns the room sickly green. I look up from the couch at Miranda's face. Her expression is startled, suspicious.

I roll onto my side and grab the phone. My little brother's name is on the screen. He has never called me in the middle of the night. Not once.

"It's my brother." A dreadful feeling.

"Don't answer it. You're busy."

"He wouldn't call me unless it was serious." The phone is on its fourth ring.

"What can you do? He is wherever he is, and you are here."

I look at her. Man, this girl is *cold*.

I press answer.

A voice rushes out like water under pressure. "*Korby*. Oh, oh, I'm so glad you answered. I don't know what to do." His voice is frantic, the way people sound on 911 calls.

I sit up. Sober. "What's the matter, Keeg?"

"It's Joncee. He's burning up. He's got a fever of 102, and it won't go down . . . Me and Jayme are on our way to the hospital right now. I don't know why I'm calling. I just called Mom and Dad. We don't know what to do."

My little brother is crying. Panicked. I don't know what to say. "You're in the car right now?" is the best I can do.

"Yes. With Jayme and Joncee." There is a rustling sound, and I hear my brother saying off the phone, "Oh, my sweet boy. Oh my good sweet boy."

"Keegan. What's going on? Joncee has a fever and you're taking him to the hospital? How far away is it?"

"Forty minutes!" comes his desperate reply. "Korby, he's burning up. We're so scared."

I am at a complete loss.

Joncee was born with a kind of cancer called *retinoblastoma* and started chemotherapy three weeks into his life. That was more than a year ago. Ever since, he's oscillated between sickness and not-quite-sick, while

Keegan and his wife, Jayme, do the best they can. But never has there been anything like this. An emergency.

"I love you. I love Jayme. I love Joncee. It will be okay." I hardly believe what I'm saying.

He says, "Okay. I love you, too. Pray for us."

I say, "Okay. Keep me posted." We hang up.

I stare at the phone. "Keep me posted?" I ask out loud. I look at Miranda. "Keep me posted. I am a shitty brother."

She is watching me, not unkindly. She pulls back her hair, holding a bobby pin in her mouth. "That sucks about your nephew. I'm sorry. But I mean, what are you supposed to do?"

"I don't know." I lay back down on the couch and look at the ceiling and think about the scene that is playing out at this moment on a desert road in southern California. A crowded little car. A baby with a fever hot enough to cause brain damage. Two parents who love their child more than their own lives, crazy with fear. My brother speeding, worrying, desperate enough to call me from fifteen hundred miles away.

So, I do the only thing I can. Still laying on my back, I say, "Dear Lord, you know I never pray and I don't even know how to, but I'm going to try because my brother needs you right now. At this moment—"

"That's not how you pray," comes a voice. I open my eyes. Miranda is sitting on the floor in lotus position, her palms laying open on her lap. She says, "Go like this. It would probably be best if we began with a chant I learned awhile back." She starts humming. She is wearing no clothes.

I feel myself starting to be sick. I run to the bathroom. I vomit. I keep picturing my baby nephew in his car seat in the back of that car.

I come back to the dirty, tan Goodwill couch and kneel down. Miranda seems to have momentarily vanished.

"*Lord.* This moment, I am here, a sinner and fool, but I come to you right now not for me but for my brother, who is your good and faithful servant. Please, please, please, come down from heaven and be with that little family in that little car . . ."

It takes about this long, and suddenly I am praying harder than I've ever prayed in my life, tears pouring out of my eyes and dripping onto the ratty couch.

"*God of heaven and earth*, I am begging you with everything in me to touch that baby. Not tomorrow. Not in a week. But *right now*. Oh lord oh lord oh lord please in this moment hear my prayer, the prayer of a bad man I know, but I love my brother and I know he loves you with all of his heart. He is one of the only truly good people I know, and right now he needs you."

I pray for about ten minutes. I say everything I know how to say, and then I don't know what else to say so I say it all over again. I sit for a minute with my eyes closed, praying silently, and when I open them, Miranda is sitting on the couch. Tears are streaming down her face.

"You really love your brother."

Then I know what to do. I pick up the phone and call Keegan back. He answers. He seems more calm. His voice is even.

"How's is going now, Keeg?" My voice is all ridiculous and breaky.

"It's okay. We're about twenty minutes away and me and Jayme are just giving everything to God. He's got it now."

I say, "He does. But would you mind if I prayed with you for a sec?"

"That would be great." We are not a super emotional family, but immediately he is crying, and I am praying all over again, praying harder than I had a moment before, because Keegan is praying too now, and I can feel a weird power through the phone.

"Oh Lord, touch this baby. Touch this baby right now. Please, Lord, let your comfort and love descend onto this little soul and make him well. Please Father, if you've ever done anything for anyone, do it now. I will do anything if you will heal this baby. Oh Lord, bring down his temperature, ease his pain. He is an innocent, Lord. He has done nothing to deserve the pain he suffers, please, Lord, help him, help him now." Through the phone I can hear Jayme saying, "Yes, Lord, yes, Lord." My brother taking gasping, sniffling breaths while he says amen.

Keegan prays, and then Jayme prays, and then I tell them I love them and they say the same. We hang up.

I lay my face down on the couch for about ten seconds. Then I sit up.

"Not good enough," I hear myself say. I grab the phone and scroll through it until I find my parent's number. I hit send and put the phone to my ear and listen to it ring.

"Hello?" says my mom in a sleepy voice. It's after four in the morning.

"Mom. It's me, Number One (her nickname for her me). Have you talked to Keegan?"

"Oh, Korby. We are afraid."

"I know. Me too . . . can we pray about it?"

A pause.

"Let me wake your father up." I hear her off the phone say "Lewis, it's Korby. He wants to pray for Joncee." She says into the phone, "Wait a second. Dad is getting on the phone in the living room."

I hear a click, and my dad's kind and solid voice comes. "Hi, Korb. I'm glad you want to pray for your brother."

I didn't think it was possible, but I pray harder now than I had the other two times, because this was my dad, and my dad is something close to a holy man. He prays and mountains move. I hear him take a breath on the phone, and in a quiet, steady voice, he says, "Oh Father, Oh Father" while I pray for my family, and my mom says, "Yes, Lord; oh please, Jesus." And I picture my baby nephew with closed eyes, and I picture big, kind hands brushing back the wispy blonde hair from his face, and I picture baby Joncee opening his eyes. And then I just picture him laughing. Happy. A happy baby.

At this point, the couch is wet, and the back of my head is hurting from crying so much, and I feel surrounded by an endless sea of love. For my brother and his wife and my nephew, for my parents. For God.

After we all pray — me, then my dad, then my mom — my mom says it is going to be fine. She knows it. We say I love you and goodbye. I hang up the phone.

The room is still dark, but I can see Miranda with two thick lines of mascara streaking down her face, looking a lot like the crazy person who lives in the house with the broken TVs and the crooked Dali painting hanging from a bent nail.

I say, "I think I'm supposed to go."

"Okay," she says. "Thank you."

I let myself out and get into the car and drive about 400 feet down the road. Then I get out and, in an act I have not done before or since, I lay down in someone's front yard and look at the stars and thank the Lord for my family and for prayer. I say thank you, thank you, over and over until I fall asleep.

16. PEEING MY PANTS AT THE HIPSTER COFFEE SHOP

I DON'T REALLY ENJOY humiliating myself. I don't. But sometimes I make a poor choice, which leads to an unfortunate but potentially entertaining episode.

The following is particularly damaging to my ego, but if I died tomorrow and the story wasn't told, the world would be missing out. So here you go, world.

Okay.

About two weeks ago, I contacted a young acquaintance in the industry about setting up an informal meeting. She had done work for an artist I really admire, and I wondered if she might share with me some of the things she did for that artist, with the intent that maybe I could hire her services to further my own cause.

She agreed on the time, and we decided to meet at Fido.

At the time, Fido was enjoying a position at the top of the local hot beverage hierarchy. It was the buzzing beehive of Nashville hipsterdom. When I first moved to town, I sat at a table by the window for hours at a time, because it reminded me of Seattle and the coffee was good and the wifi reliable and I had seen Jack White and his supermodel girlfriend there the first time I went.

Vis-à-vis my industry meeting: I am excited. I like the girl on a personal level, because she seems put-together and enthusiastic. Plus, we shared a meal once and it just clicked. Okay, abounding good vibes. Great.

I have just finished a four-hour rehearsal and arrive maybe five minutes late. I wait in line and order not coffee but a beer. It is late in the day, and I can't drink coffee after four.

In hindsight, it was not one of my best decisions. I had been drinking water all throughout my rehearsal. So this was like more water.

I sit at her table, and we talk for a long time about stuff not related to music, the way people do. But the more we talk, the more I have to shift my weight around. I should get up but I don't. I don't know why I don't.

We finally get to the point, and I say well, I don't have the momentum of artist x right now, but I think I will, and if that happens, I won't be able to keep up. And when that time comes, I will need someone talented and driven and who believes in me to help me keep the ship sailing smoothly. I think I can see a moment of disappointment mixed with annoyance flash on her face, but I am being forthright and honest. So maybe I am imagining things.

At this point, I really should excuse myself. But I think we are about to part and, it's always awkward when someone gets up to use the bathroom when everyone else is about to leave. So I decide to hold on.

Somehow, we keep talking; details, bigger life questions. The conversation moves along through three more topics. We start chatting about the first time we went to see a live show. Ten minutes pass. Fifteen.

I am in agony at this point. But now I really can't excuse myself, because we are *so* about to leave. I can feel it. There is nothing to do but hang on. I think I'm keeping it cool from the chin up. My face registers none of the alarming urgency of my lower torso. We talk. I listen.

At last, we are ready to go. When we stand up, I realize the situation is desperate. All I can think about is my immediate bodily need, but I am with someone I don't know that well and also in a public place where everyone is wearing tight jeans and white belts. I am alone here. I move carefully.

As I walk her to the rear exit of Fido, I can't really even form complete sentences. I can feel my body wanting to twist and contort like a kinked hose. So. This is what a bladder-induced meltdown looks like.

I have no idea what I have been saying for these last thirty terrible seconds, but it must not have been very confidence-inspiring, because as I give her the industry-approved half-hug of goodbye the look I see on her face hits the mark somewhere between disapproval and disgust, and it's just too much. I am suddenly six years old, sitting in class in the third row, wetting my pants.

I watch her walk through the door, and I just stand there with a horrified smile fixed on my face. Is this really happening? I look down and watch the blue in my jeans grow darker. Yes, it is.

For some reason, I don't move. It's no lie the people who wet their pants feel a strange and comforting warmth. I stand there like a man transfixed. I try to remain calm. Then I casually walk to the door that has a big M on it.

After a minute or so there, I walk slowly through the coffee shop, looking appropriately disinterested. It is not the first time someone in Fido wore jeans with two kinds of blue on them, right?

I walk out the front door, around the corner to my little grey car. I pop open the door and sit down in the driver's seat. Not a very pleasant feeling there.

On the way home, I send a text to my coffee mate to say thanks for the hang. No answer.

Nor was there an answer to the email I sent a few days later.

On my gravestone, please inscribe the phrase "he meant well" in arial font. Bold type.

17. HER IMPOSSIBLE HEART

ONCE UPON A TIME, there was a young girl whose heart was so big, it barely fit in her chest. It rubbed against the inside of her ribcage and made her skin itch. "Allergies," she would say when people asked. "Eczema." She was shy about her big heart.

And the sound! The steady thump of her heartbeat was so loud, you could hear it when you waited in line behind her at the grocery store. You would turn and look at this little girl with strawberry hair and wonder at the big sound that came out of her. It was like a bass drum in a marching band wrapped in a blanket. It was a faraway sound.

She would pretend not to notice, holding a pack of gum in her small hand, waiting her turn. She was sixteen, with skinny arms and glasses and smooth alabaster skin and this extra-large heart that somehow had been placed inside an extra-small carrying case.

Sometimes, it annoyed her. She would be sitting on the couch after school, watching TV and suddenly she would start thinking about her pet chinchilla that had died when she was six. Or the old woman she had seen the day before yesterday crossing the street so slowly the other cars had had to wait on her. She would picture the old woman's withered face or remember the way it felt to pet the chinchilla, and her heart would ache, and she would sit on the couch and cry. She didn't mean to.

She was terrible in libraries, at tests. Anytime you were supposed to be quiet. That's when you really noticed how loud her banging heartbeat was. It was distracting. You couldn't think.

Even still, you loved her. Everyone loved her. It was impossible not to. She would look at you and you would feel like something was right in the world. The world had made this lovely girl. There she was, right in front of you.

Of all the people that loved her, it was her father who loved her the most. He would make packed lunches and lean over her homework and take her to the movies. He knew how to make her sandwiches the way she liked them, how much mustard. He would drive her to the park to feed the ducks, and, later, to the mall and the movies. He had done this since she was a baby, and he would do it every day until she grew up and went away from him. Is what he thought.

But he was wrong, because one day she got very sick. Her great big heart was so big, her little body couldn't keep itself together. Her father took her to the doctor. Then to the hospital. The doctors crowded around her and were sad. They didn't know what to do.

But there she was in a hospital bed, with the tubes and the needles coming out of her, and still this heart was beating away like a kick drum.

One night turned into two, into ten. Her father stayed with her the whole time, reading her favorite books to her with funny glasses on his nose, making up stories, holding her hand when they gave her shots. At night, he would sit in a chair beside her bed and tell her all his memories of her, when she was a baby, when she started school. They would look at pictures together, old photo albums of vacations and birthdays. He would tell her how much he loved her, how badly he wished he could fix her. That he would give her his heart, that he would give her anything. He would hold the little hand and watch her sleep and listen to her heartbeat banging, away, and he would pray, even though he didn't know how to do it or who he was praying to, because he loved her so terribly.

It was late one night when her heart started beating more quietly; that's when he knew. He barely noticed it at first, but after a few hours, he was sure. Her heartbeat was quieter. It was still loud, too loud, but less loud. He sat up and watched her carefully. In an hour, it had grown quieter still. Just a tom tom now, a hand drum.

He drew near her and laid his head down on her chest and listened to her heartbeat. It was the sound of her life, this life he loved more than his own. It was music. Music that had played so loud for so long and was now just a little rhythm. Brushes on a snare.

The two of them here now, alone in the softy lit room with her quiet music.

He wished he could hold that heartbeat in his hands. He wished he could do anything. He lay his helpless head on her heart and listened to the song play softer and softer.

She had been asleep, but she was awake now. Her eyes on his, watching him listen to her. She had stopped being able to talk days ago, but her eyes shined, said to him, thank you Daddy. I love you. In this moment, I couldn't have asked for anything more than to be with you, right here, right now. Thank you for everything.

for Cyan and Scarpati

18. MANBOY AND THE MAFIA TABLE

THEY WAITED FOR A LONG time to be seated. Some of them drifted over to the bar to buy a whiskey, to pass time and make the talking easier. Others stood by the entrance in their wool coats and scarves, hunching their shoulders against the southern cold that rushed in every time someone opened the door. Their hard shoes made clicking sounds on the tile floor as they shuffled around. Simon was with them. He was one of the ones waiting by the door.

It was just a few days after the New Year, and the room was crowded with faces still fattened with holiday cheer. Waiters skirted around the black tables carrying trays of pizza and dark beer. Christmas music dropped from the ceiling speakers and shivered in the air like old tinsel.

Simon stood with his hands in his pockets and watched a couple at a table near him. Several uneaten crusts lay on their plates, and they both were leaning back in the chairs like athletes exhausted from a workout. At an adjacent booth, a group of three men and a woman huddled around a pitcher of golden beer. They were talking in low voices until the woman by the window suddenly shrieked in laughter, horse-like. Her mouth a huge oval. The man sitting next to her turned away and looked uncomfortable.

While he watched, a waiter walked past them, carrying a tray loaded with drinks. As he bent down to begin passing them out, a mug of beer slid off the edge of the tray and crashed into a wet glassy mess on the floor. It made an exciting sound, and everyone turned to look.

Almost immediately, a girl appeared with a mop and a dustpan and began cleaning it up. When she bent over to push the bits of glass into the pan Simon could see a faded inky tattoo at the place where her back met her backside. “Fabulous.”

Sometimes, in crowded rooms, when Simon wanted to run away but couldn’t, he liked to close his eyes and listen to the Whole Sound. The Whole Sound was a game he invented a long time ago where you try to take in all the present noises without hearing any one noise in particular. It could be very calming in trying situations, even if it was the social equivalent of an ostrich shoving its head in the sand.

Simon closed his eyes. At first the bits, and pieces of conversation came at him like severed limbs… *She’s a total bitch. These shoes at Ross for seventeen dollars . .*

. I can't believe he likes that... Wasn't as good as the first one where . . . Time I noticed I had lost weight was when Jack looked at me and said . . . But then he took a deep breath and relaxed his ear drums—he could almost feel them lean back in his head—and it was like a Jackson Pollock painting took shape, crackling in the air. The hum of distant voices and passing cars made warm soft shades for the bright lights of glass and laughter to lay on. Clicking shoes punched holes in the canvas and the grease sizzling in the kitchen broke into applause with its million clapping hands. It was irreverent and frenzied and glad to be alive, as though the whole of God's sacred circus had wandered into Mafiaoza's and sat down for dinner. All these people with paintbrushes, each unique, flinging color everywhere with wild abandon. Simon listened for a long time, unaware that a smile teased at the corner of his lips. It was a thing lovely for an ostrich to behold.

Suddenly, he heard a girl's voice say, "It's the mafia table. That's why it's taking so long." He recognized the voice as belonging to one of his party. The painting snapped off its mount on the wall and broke into pieces and disappeared.

Mafia table. Even though he wondered what it was, he knew he wouldn't ask. Instead, he opened his eyes to slits and let just a little bit of light in. *Easy now, Simon. You've been back in there awhile now.*

With his eyes cracked open like that, the blurred shapes that moved in the half-light made him feel like he was in a room full of ghosts. Like that ride at

Disneyland where the pictures stretch in the elevator and then you look into the mirrors and there's a blurry green goblin sitting on your shoulder.

Simon looked around through the slits. From in here, the sacred circus was a bit too much. The laughter too loud. He swore he saw a clown. He wished he had something to hold onto. He wished The Girl hadn't gone to the bar and left him. Maybe he should join her. *No, people need to do things they're afraid of. You must be brave, Simon.* He took a deep breath and opened his eyes all the way.

There was a young man standing almost in front of him, not talking with anyone. He was a Manboy, meaning he would have been an adult in any generation other than this one. Long ago, a self-respecting man of twenty-six would have balked at the thought of purposefully dressing like an androgynous child. But in this, our age of protracted adolescence, if you are somewhat slender and creative-minded, you dress in tight, casual clothes that draw attention to your sexuality. Manboy.

This one was wearing a little pea coat with a broken catch on the second buckle. Simon took this in. It was a comfort, he decided. You are not the only imperfect one, said the buckle.

Simon felt a nudge of confidence. He could see himself trying to talk. He thought about what would be a good thing to say. He straightened his own coat. He checked his phone.

One more deep breath and he turned to the Manboy in the pea coat with the broken buckle and introduced himself. He said his name in a friendly way so the Manboy would like him. Manboy said his own name and when they shook hands in the white people style, the handshake was firm and confident. Okay, I respect you, said Simon to himself.

They made small talk, and while they did that, Simon did what he always did, which was try to figure out what kind of person he was talking to.

For one, Manboy was what you would call svelte. He was of average height, but his frame was that of a boxer's. He looked fit. His short brown hair poked up in the center, and thick eyebrows arched over his eyes so gracefully Simon bet they were plucked. And apart from the broken buckle, the Manboy looked like he had just stepped out of an H&M. Still, he was hard not to like. His manner was easygoing and friendly in a way that defied his manicured appearance.

They were talking about current events, one of Simon's favorite subjects, when Manboy asked him a question about something he was wearing. His scarf, where he got it. Only then did Simon notice they were both wearing scarves. It always annoyed him when he wasn't dazzlingly original, so this was one of those annoying times. I guess I am a Manboy too, he thought.

At last, The Girl appeared, carrying two beers. As she passed him one, someone made a flattering comment about her hair, and she turned and smiled. He knew she was genuinely pleased. She liked her hair. He liked her hair too. It was the color of honey. It smelled like flowers.

As she talked to a girl beside him, he looked at her and pressed the mute button in his head so he could watch better. She had large blue eyes that were somehow always faraway looking, even when she was looking right at you. Her cheekbones were high and prominent, and her faced tapered to a point below her mouth which most people would call a chin but that was too plain a word for the subtle orchestration of flesh and bone that comprised this southerly place. The whole arrangement was just west of classic.

She was the most beautiful girl he knew. But his admiration of her was only partly due to the way she looked. There were many faces which could be described as pretty, but the power of a face was not its surface but what was behind it, what illuminated it. Her spiritual backlight was what set her apart. It was a face of composure and deep feeling, both at once. It was a powerful face.

She caught him watching her. She wrinkled her nose, said mockingly, "Stop looking at me, creepy man."

"I can't."

"You will," she said. "I demand you stop. It's rude."

"I never said I had good manners."

"Not true. You tell me how polite you are all the time. You brag about it."

"Sometimes I have to point out the things you miss, darling."

She took a sip. "Well, it's annoying. You should give me more credit. I notice more than you think. I notice everything."

"What do you notice?"

"Well for starters, I see you're having one of your dramatic episodes."

"How do you know?"

"How does a deer know the storm is coming?"

"I'm not sure it does. Sometimes the deer is wrong."

"The deer is never wrong." She looked at him flatly. "You had your eyes closed, Stormy."

"I might just be saving up."

"Oh, I'm sure of that."

He wondered what she meant, being sure of that. He took a long sip. He liked it when she was mysterious. She was mysterious all the time. That was probably his favorite thing about her. She was talented and beautiful and kind, true enough, but on God's green earth, there was no greater delight than a mysterious woman.

He had known other beautiful women before who could be described as mysterious, but they were only that way from a distance, until he talked to them awhile. Then they were known, and that was the sad end of it. But here was a new situation. He had been courting The Girl for a year now, and still he was often surprised at what she might say next. At first it baffled him, because she was obviously not trying to be coy.

She simply *was* coy. She was the incarnation of effortless mystery. What luck he had found her. He felt his eyes water.

Now she was talking with the other scarved Manboy. He was telling her about his band. He was flirting with her, saying something about being a huge fan of Elliot Smith. Saying he loved the song "Angel in the Snow." She laughed and said how much she liked that song too. Maybe this joker needed to be watched a little more carefully.

Now he was singing the song to her. He held his invisible microphone in front of his face and closed his eyes and whined.

"I'd say you make a perfect
Angel in the snow
All crushed out on the way you are
Better stop before it goes too far!"

She sang the last line with him in harmony. More laughing. She caught Simon's eye. The look said, "Don't be unpleasant, darling; it's just a spot of fun." Simon smiled back. He started to think about breaking the rest of Manboy's buckles.

The hostess arrived to announce the mafia table was ready. The group collected itself and followed her across the dining room to a dark alcove in the back. There, sandwiched between two high walls coated in red velvet wallpaper, lay a long wooden table, polished glossy walnut brown. People began to slide into the booth until all sixteen of them were rooted in place shoulder to shoulder. A single lamp hung low from the ceiling, dripping a smoky yellow light that fell hard on their faces and exaggerated shadows at the cheekbone and eye socket. Simon and The Girl were the last in line, and so took the last two spots, closest to the aisle. He on the outside, she one seat in. Manboy, the singing scarf-wearer, somehow conspired to be the other person sitting beside her.

As he pulled off his coat The Girl leaned over and kissed him on the cheek. He turned and gave her a wry smile. Doing his best Goodfellas he said, "This ain't no place for affection, Gina. The fellas and I came here to discuss business."

She narrowed her eyes. "Oh, Eddie," she said, "You're always talking business. Leave it alone for one night, yeah?"

"You know what? You're right. Tonight is for pleasure and pleasure only!" Simon leaned forward on his elbows and surveyed the group. All of them were artists. Most of them were talented. None of them were famous. The table was so large that Simon could hear nothing of what was being said at the far side, but he could see people saying nice things to each other in the way well-meaning acquaintances do. There were teeth in the smiles, and eyes flashed to the whites. Many of them barely knew each other. Some of them were even rivals, if only in secret.

Manboy piped up. "I would like to raise a toast."

The group ceased to acquaint.

His lifted glass was full of white wine, yellowing in its close proximity to the overhead lamp. He said, "I am new to town. It does not matter where I came from. But in the short time I have been here, I note with admiration and respect a feature that is singular and constant among the creative people who call this place home. Never have I visited a city where there was to be found such a combination of talent and heart. Most places have one or the other. Actually, most places have none of either, but here, here in this southern City of Music, I find a people for whom it is not enough to sing in tune. One must have something to say . . . To talent and heart!"

"Talent and heart!" returned the chorus. Glasses chimed. People leaned across and over to touch drinks and salute the ones who lay beyond polite reach.

Simon felt a stirring. This one was smart. He didn't like it.

He remembered once when he was in college, there was a girl in his class who was always saying interesting things, things that impressed the professor, things that were genuinely interesting (instead of a pretend kind of academic interesting). The class was on the Foundations of Western Civilization or something and this girl knew the Greek poets and playwrights by name and was always bringing up stuff that Simon was impressed with and even occasionally moved by, but his annoyance at her virtuosity overpowered any attraction he would have had. No, it wasn't that, now that he thought of it. What actually bothered him was the professor liked her more than him. That was the problem. He just liked to win.

Simon cleared his throat. "A very touching sentiment from our young friend here." He said it slowly and with a slurred New Jersey Italian accent. "We are all duly flattered you have found our company so inspiring. My girl, Gina, says she has herself never seen a young man with such a combination of good looks and manners. I must assume you're Italian?"

Manboy looked at Simon, his eyes narrowed indistinguishably. "Sicilian on my mother's side," he said, adding, "from the Old Country."

"Of course," Simon wheezed. "The Don speaks very highly of your family. You must have some real talent, rising through the ranks as fast as you did."

The look on Manboy's face said, I have no idea what you're talking about. Simon didn't know, either. He wasn't sure what was happening here.

"What can I say?" said Manboy at last. "I saw where I wanted to go and I went there."

Simon took a slow, exaggerated breath, like an old fat man would. "You're ambitious. I like that. Isn't he ambitious, Gina?"

"Almost as ambitious as you, Eddie." Good girl. He loved this girl.

Simon felt his heart beating faster. Usually he was

the last person to involve himself in an open confrontation. But he had somehow tricked himself into this. The Girl was here. His friends were here. This kid was not going to waltz into his life and stir up any kind of disruption worth noticing. That was not going to happen.

Simon leveled a slow gaze at the place where Manboy was sitting. Simon said, "That fella you work for—the tall skinny. Archie? Archie Knuckles. There's a crafty one. He knows his racket, and he runs it real good. Ain't afraid to do what has to be done, you know what I mean?"

"Archie's the best." Manboy was now looking at Simon with open hostility. The lamp began to swing imperceptibly over them.

"No," said Simon, looking directly at the Manboy. "Archie is not the best. The Don is the best, and the Don does not like it when his interests are threatened by tall skinnies from the Old Country."

"Eddie, you're makin our guests feel uncomfortable." It was, The Girl saying this, still in character. He looked at her, and her eyes were almost glowing with alarm. She hated scenes. He hated scenes too. He didn't know what was happening or why he was doing it, but he was nothing if not someone who saw a thing through, every time, to the very end.

"Gina, I'm a lucky man. I don't know what I'd do without you."

Now, Simon turned and stuck his pointer finger in Manboy's face. "But you. You tell Archie Knuckles he better stay out of the Don's way, 'less he wants a visit from Lucky Eddie. The Don has been very patient thus far, but patience is like lighter fluid, you know? It has a way of running out."

While he had been speaking, Simon had withdrawn a red Bic lighter. Now he drew his thumb back over the metal wheel, and the whole table watched a white glow flicker at the end of the cylinder. Simon drew the flame up to light the imaginary cigarette hanging from his mouth. He flicked the lighter off and and touched his lips with the two fingers of his other hand, pulling the cigarette away and slowly exhaling a cloud of invisible smoke in Manboy's face.

Manboy turned bright red. No one breathed.

When bad things happen, they happen fast. Manboy made a sudden violent motion, bringing his wine glass down across the left side of Simon's face. It broke on impact and cut into the flesh of Simon's cheek. The shattering glass made a tinkling sound, and Simon felt his skin part and his face flush wet and hot. A red liquid spilled out onto the table, more than he would have thought.

Simon rose to defend himself, but at the same time he wanted to laugh. It felt so good. Something real was happening. Even as he brought his forearm up to meet Manboy's nose, he wasn't angry. He wanted to hug him.

He missed the nose. The chin instead. Man, I suck at fighting, he thought.

The glancing blow pushed Manboy back into the

booth on a nice girl with a green felt coat that Simon didn't know. Now the lamp was swinging wildly on its cord, rocking the shadows back and forth and making it hard to see what was happening.

The girl with the green coat pushed Manboy back up. For a moment, the two looked at each other. Simon and Manboy.

Then Manboy reached over and steadied the lamp. Everything stopped moving. He looked at Simon.

"I didn't mean to do that. It's bleeding pretty bad, man."

"Well, I was the one who blew smoke in your face."

The rest of the guests wore their faces like plates of white china. Everyone wanted it to go away. Simon felt bad. This was his fault. He had just gotten carried away.

He put his fingers on the cheek and withdrew them to look. The color was the brightest red he'd ever seen. "I'm sorry," he said. "You seem like a very nice person, Manboy. I am on antibiotics, and it makes me wonky when I drink wine." He wasn't on antibiotics and he hadn't been drinking wine, but he thought everyone needed to hear some kind of explanation. "Now, I will wash this out at home."

"I'll take you, Stormy." It was The Girl. She had champagne on her dress, and her face had little speckles of his blood on it. She picked her purse up off the floor.

They both turned and left Manboy and their stunned friends at the table, walking down the aisle to the front of the restaurant, where he had seen the girl with the "Fabulous" tattoo sweep up bits of glass. People were staring, and Simon felt self-conscious but then the staring people helped him remember something so he gently took The Girl's arm and turned and walked back to the mafia table.

"Sorry. Would someone mind taking our picture? This probably won't happen again for awhile."

A pause, then, "I'll take it." Manboy.

He put his arm around The Girl. There was blood on his coat, but her dress was ruined anyway. The Girl pressed a napkin up to the cut on his cheek, but Simon pushed it away. "In a second," he said. This is an Important Moment.

They faced the crowd of fourteen people pressed tightly together in the long booth called Mafia Table, and Simon smiled a big one he saved for only the best occasions.

Manboy snapped the photo.

19. BIRD CRUSH

IT WAS JUST ANOTHER DAY and another evening and another evening run. The air thick with sweat and slightly rotten. A haze of clouds graying the sky. Pieces of pinkish light here and there. The muted boom of thunder from a storm two counties over.

He set out like he always did, stumbling out of the front door in red shorts and white shoes and a faded Orange Crush baseball cap. Now across the front yard, pushing through the laziness and reluctance that always began the run, feeling his way toward the rhythm that would carry him through the neighborhood and down to the muddy river and back to his house.

He reached the street and looked down as though through a movie lens, watching the feet enter the bottom of the frame, white blurred shoes stabbing the street left and right and left and right and left.

There were children outside—first the ones whose names he knew and then, a block later, strangers. Sprinklers clicking over lawns and flower beds. The insect swell of cicadas overhead. The hissing sound they made, like snakes in the trees.

The feet now full in their rhythm, the feel of the run changing from a push to the pull that would carry him all the way to the river. His mind began to settle into the hushed and secret room that is the runner's pleasure. A clean white room with many windows and no furniture.

A steep hill approached. He tucked his chin down onto his chest and saw the blue shirt he wore was beginning to darken in the middle. He listened to his breath, the way it sounded. Like an animal wind. It had a rhythm of its own, separate from the rhythm of the feet. He listened to the breath-rhythm and the feet-rhythm. They were out of time, not even close. And yet he was producing them both. This was a worthy mystery.

He sailed along in his sweaty reverie that was one part health and one part psychosis, and he came to an intersection and turned left onto an unfamiliar street. Different houses, different children playing. Different sprinklers. But still sprinklers and still children and houses and cicadas and the thunder in the distance and the grey hazy clouds overhead and the off-kilter rhythm of the feet and the breath. Nothing really changes, really.

But he was wrong. Things do change.

He ran along this new sidewalk on the unfamiliar street, and before he reached the first new intersection, he saw something unusual. Something in the street was leaping and tumbling and fluttering wildly, like a child's toy. Alive and grey and broken. Careening back and forth like a drunk, strange and alarming. He stopped running so as to watch it from a distance.

It was a bird, a pigeon, trying and failing and trying again to fly.

Breathing heavily and sweating darkness into his shirt, he approached the fluttering mess like it was a danger to him. It looked like it had been run over by a car somehow. Was its back broken? Its body was the shape of a banana. But maybe that's what pigeons looked like and people just didn't notice. He wasn't sure. What was clear was that something was wrong. Emergency room wrong. The bird was making its way through the sacred eternal battle, the walk through the valley of the shadow of death.

He didn't know what to do. What could he do? Take it to a veterinarian? That was not in the cards. But he watched the little animal's struggle in the darkening light, and he knew at once he could not leave it.

He walked up for a closer look, leaning forward like a detective. The bird looked at him sideways with a single orange eye, a perfect mandarin circle center-punched with a small black dot, animated yet with life and hope and hurt. Its chest was heaving.

He approached carefully. The bird stilled. He heard himself say a few soft words, like he was talking to a sleeping baby. "Oh little one." The pigeon flapped its wings uselessly. They were broken.

His hands reached down, and there were more soft words, and he gently folded the wings back at the bird's side, and the bird allowed him to do this. He lifted it with all the delicacy in him. "Oh honey," he said.

They were in the middle of the street, and the street was empty and the sky yet darker and still grey. He carried the bird, warm and heavy and heaving in his hands, and he walked to a small green place above the sidewalk. He set the pigeon down in the grass, and the moment he did this the bird leapt and fluttered and tumbled down into the street and landed with wings everywhere and its head sideways on the pavement and the one orange eye still watching him.

He jumped down and picked up the dying bird and apologized and carried it in his cupped hands to the grassy place, and this time he held it with one hand while the other touched its smooth, stoney head. The eye blinked and watched him, and he said over and over, "Oh I'm sorry oh I'm sorry," because the bird was dying and these were its last minutes in this world and they both knew it. "Oh honey I am sorry this is happening to you." And he was. He was sorry this feathered innocent must tremble before him in fear and confusion, and he was sorry that even though the bird and he were together, one against the other, they were really miles and oceans apart, he squarely in the land of the living and the bird fast disappearing from this earth, once and forever. He could hold the bird and tell it he loved it and even cry for it, but the unhappy bird was in this moment alone and alone utterly. None can go there otherwise. The suffering must be unspeakably intense right now, and yet here it was, bearing its misfortune with all the grace of a humble creature made by God and given dignity and perfect beauty even now at this most terrible of moments.

At some point, there were tears that came out of him which he didn't notice except that one splashed on the pigeon's small head, which made it twist around again. A car passed and slowed to gaze at the spectacle of a grown man sweating and crying and sitting in the grass holding a twitching bird.

He was not the most religious person in the world, but he didn't know what to do, so he prayed to God for the little bird's life, thanking God for its years of flying under the sun and feasting on worms, or whatever pigeons ate, and then he thanked God that he had been the one who ran by, that he had turned at the intersection. Because what if he had not? The little bird dying in terror out in the street like a beggar. It would have been a grave sin.

The bird started shaking. He guessed it was going into shock. He held its warm body against his chest, sitting cross-legged in the grass and saying, "I'm sorry," and "God loves you," which he knew was foolish, but it didn't matter. They sat there together for some fifteen minutes, he with the bird and the bird with him and night falling fast. Finally, the head turned once again toward him and the orange eye looked at him with a new expression of surrender and sadness, and the eyelid started blinking rapidly. The pigeon shuddered in his hands once more with a solemn violence, and at last he felt its life flow out of its body for all time, and then the body was calm and warm, and the eyelid stopped blinking, and he was just a sweaty man holding a dead bird.

It was almost completely dark, and a streetlight yellowed the sidewalk below him. He carried the bird to an empty lot and set it down and said one more prayer for dead animals everywhere and stood up. Its orange eyes were closed. He looked at it for a long time, because he knew the next time he ran this way the bird would be gone. He bent down once more and pulled its wings apart so it looked like it was flying.

Somewhere in the struggle, the cicadas had stopped and the thunder had stopped and there were no stars because the haze was the same in the night sky as the day. He couldn't run any longer, so instead he walked home as though from a funeral, where the living feel pity for the dead and the dead are left behind and the living are not the same as they were before.

Above the clouds and in secret, a meteor shower covered the earth in streaking bits of light that burned shamelessly in the sky once and for all time and then disappeared forever.

20. THE COOL GREEN HILLS OF EARTH ARE NOT ENOUGH

"**I ANNOY MYSELF** so much it is painful" is what Simon thought as he pressed and held the delete key and watched the cursor zip backwards until all the words he had just written disappeared. This story was going nowhere. It was about a depressed person who has decided to give up once and for all, and so he drives his barely-running station wagon to the gun store only to find out he has to wait three days before he can buy a gun.

But the story had many problems. One was that he had determined long ago only to write about the things he knew, and the truth was that he knew nothing about guns—how much they cost, how much they weighed, what it felt like when you pull the hammer back. Even the phrase, "when you pull the hammer back" rang false, because he had never done it, not even once.

The other problem was that chapter eight was a lovely story about a botched suicide, and the thought of repeating himself was more disagreeable than the act itself. The subject had been covered in its explicit form, and now the author must move on. Everyone has problems. Get over it.

The truth was that he wasn't about to kill himself with a gun or a jump from a tall building or anything else. For one, he knew the feeling of abject despair would pass—it had come and gone many times before, and so there was every reason to believe it would go again. For two, he still liked a few things. He liked the taste of a pale beer from the bottle, he liked the sensation of touching that girl's skin—the coolness of it, the cleanliness. Her words when she spoke to him, the sound of her voice, the strange mystery of her. He liked the feeling of playing music, the sound of an open G chord with the D on the B string fretted. He liked making things up with his mind. There were too many pleasures. They were not lost. They would come again.

Simon thought this through, watching the cursor blink on the screen of the laptop. Then, he stood up from the bench in the forested park where he had been writing his bad story and set the computer down beside him. He took a deep breath. He ran his right hand through his dirty hair. He listened and looked and was still. There were birds around, but he couldn't see them. It was all sounds. The light was there, though, the yellow-green light distilled through the late summer leaves into a color so pure it was like the beginning of time. If he wasn't wearing clothes, it could have been ten thousand years ago.

But he was wearing clothes, blue jeans that cost a fortune and were made by Asian children or something. Some kind of shirt he had bought at a designer store years ago. And, of course, those exquisite shoes. Who could think about suicide wearing shoes like that? He was a free man in the prime of life. He could breathe. He could do push-ups. It was amazing.

Still, there was the problem of the story. A deadline loomed. Did it matter that it was a manufactured deadline? No. That no one was actually waiting for this story was of small import. Simon lived in a generation of entrepreneurs. He was his own boss, and the truth was that his boss was an absolute asshole when he missed his deadline, to the point of following him home and keeping him awake at night until it got done. He should have been fired years ago, but unfortunately for the boss, no one else could do the job. They were stuck with each other.

So there was Simon in the park, standing beside the bench with the ancient yellow light, and his hand now sticky from the fingers poking through his sweaty hair.

As was usually the case, he was looking for something, only he didn't know what.

Suddenly, there came through the trees and into his head a half-remembered line from another story, someone else's. What was it? Simon closed his eyes.

Hemingway. Something about courage. How life breaks everyone and the people it can't break it kills. It was something he had read ten years ago in another life, in another part of the world and now he was seized with an intense desire to find it, the book, and read the passage, so he could know if it really said what he thought it said.

He folded up the computer and began to walk across the park, following the patches of shade as he made his way toward the car.

IT IS HARD TO KNOW why people do what they do. What makes them go and seek out unknown dangers, submitting their precious lives to causes the worth of which they only barely understand? What are they hoping to find? Not everyone is like this, but some of them are. Most of them draw their pleasure from the fruits of their labor: the goal is in the repose, in the cool drink sipped in the dying light of the well-worked day. But there are an accursed few, the prophet and the misfit, who find no real pleasure in the repose. The cool green hills of earth are not enough. The very comfort of these hills is unpleasant in its pleasantness. For these unhappy men and women, the struggle is the reward. Restless in their pursuits, restless in their sleep, they search out the very thing they know they cannot find, yet hoping against hope they will find it. Pity the poor creatures! It is a terrible affliction which besets the unhappy prophet, in itself and in the mind-set it fosters: the prophet rejects the fellowship of his friends and family, sleeping alone in the dust beyond the gates of the city, telling himself he is a hero when he is not. He turns from the wine which God gave him for his pleasure and instead lies on his belly, sucking mud from the puddle, hoping to find some comfort from the grime in his teeth.

Simon pulled his barely-running station wagon into the parking lot of the used book store, found a space at the far end of the lot, cut the power. The car rocked slightly from left to right as the engine wound down. Simon unrolled the driver's side window, reached out and opened the door from the outside. He got out of the car, walked slowly across the parking lot, pulled open the glass door, and went inside.

The air was cool. He stood for a moment at the front door and looked around, orienting himself. A girl stamping books at the front counter looked over her glasses at him and asked if he needed help.

Simon asked where Hemingway was. The girl said he was buried in Sun Valley, Idaho. A pause. "I'm joking," she said. "Far aisle, over there," pointing.

Simon said thanks. He turned the corner where the girl said to go and followed the line of books down from the A's. Atwood, Beckett, Cather, Golding, ah, Hemingway.

Simon took a bent paperback copy of *A Farewell to Arms* down from the shelf and looked at the front cover. There was a picture, an engraving, of a woman looking to her right and in the background a man in a soldier's outfit, about to walk out of frame. Simon turned the book over. The back said something about how the author did more to change the style of English prose than anyone else in the twentieth century. "Very good, sir," said Simon aloud. It is good to achieve things. He turned the book again. On the side opposite the binding, in red marker, someone had written "Megan Chambers" with a big heart after her name. Simon wondered if Megan Chambers had written that or if it was the work of Megan Chambers' admirer. He opened the book.

It took a long time to find what he was looking for. He didn't know where it was. A lot of times, Hemingway wrote descriptions about action, and only once in a while would he write about what went on inside himself or make declarations about how the world was. That made it easy to do a lot of light skimming. He saw where the bomb went off, where he escaped the Italian soldiers who were executing officers for desertion. He got to the part where he and Catherine row across the lake in the storm in the night, trying to make it to Switzerland. Then Catherine had the baby, and Simon slowed down and started reading every sentence. It was a hateful tragedy. The injustice of it. The indifference of fate. The main character prayed that his love Catherine, would not die from giving birth to the baby but die she did, and took his prayers with her. It was terrible, but it was a comfort too. You are not alone, said the words. See how this ends, it is terrible, but see also how these people loved one another, what they meant to each other, that is true, too. There is much to live for, much that is precious. There is so much that is rare and beautiful, and we should be grateful for the mystery and the wonder of it and look at it and feel it and make it our own as much as we are able.

Simon closed the book. He leaned back against the bookshelf. He thought. In some ways, he was a lost person, sucking mud through his teeth, looking for God. But only in some ways. In other ways, he was maybe okay. There was hope for the old boy yet. He opened the book once more. It only took a second to find. Somehow he turned right to it.

If people bring so much courage to this world the world has to kill them to break them, so of course it kills them. The world breaks everyone and afterward many are strong at the broken places. But those that will not break it kills. It kills the very good and the very gentle and the very brave impartially. If you are none of these you can be sure it will kill you too but there will be no special hurry.

Simon went out to the car and got his computer. He walked back into the bookstore and sat down in the aisle by the Hemingways. He felt like he had something to say. He typed for awhile on his computer. A teenager with a black T-shirt and jeans and black shoes walked by, and Simon asked the teenager to take his picture.

The teenager asked why. Simon said he needed to illustrate a story he was writing. The teenager said no and moved on. Simon typed for awhile and then an older lady with dangling earrings walked by, and Simon asked her. She said okay. Simon handed her his phone which was also a camera and the woman crouched down to get a good angle.

Simon wrote the whole story out, sitting with his legs crossed in the aisle of the bookstore. He was checking it for typos when someone came by and said that the store was closing. Simon folded his computer and stood up and walked out the door he had come through. The night was warm.

21. AMPLIFIED DESIRE AND A DIRTY PEACOAT

I PLAYED A SHOW Friday night.

Sometimes I have a bad feeling while I play, and this was one of those times. For the first two songs I couldn't hear myself, then I could hear myself too much. The sound kept seesawing through the monitor in front of me on stage, and I had to pretend I wasn't miserable. Music is about many things, but one thing it's not about is pretending, so I knew the people watching me were feeling what I was feeling. Uncertainty and frustration. And I was so looking forward to this show. I had spent three weeks of extra shifts at the hotel parking cars just to pay the band. I had rehearsed everyone earlier that day, and everything was sounding like polished glass with just the right amount of jagged, and then, when it came time to play, the sound was wrong. Not just a little wrong but *on purpose* wrong. The man behind the board had it in for me, or maybe he didn't, maybe he was a student (that happens sometimes) or he just hated music, or maybe it was all my fault, like I just couldn't hear what was right in front of me. Whatever the reason, the show was bad and I knew it. I was embarrassed and disappointed and filled with an acute desire to disappear from the world.

At the end of the last song, I dropped my guitar on the stage. I had forgotten to put the amp on standby so it made a loud, tuneless crashing sound when the strings made contact with the stage. I was more embarrassed, but I acted like I meant for it to happen and walked across the room to the front door, escaping.

The air outside felt like a splash of cold water, the sweat on my face making a quick decision whether to freeze or evaporate. I walked down the steps and turned left onto the sidewalk and kept walking.

I passed the Mexican restaurant next door and looked at my reflection in the window. My whole body was steaming. Someone should take my picture, I thought.

My ears were ringing from the show, but I could still hear the honkytonks on lower Broadway buzzing and popping like an AM signal, four blocks and one universe away. I stopped and listened. Electric guitars and train rhythms. The southern version of amplified desire. I pulled the corner of my upper lip into a sneer and played a lick on air guitar and started walking again.

I rounded the corner and looked across the street at a telephone pole. One poster fastened with staples for the show I had just played. My name in bold type.

"Korby Lenker," I said out loud.

Then, I shouted, "Korby Lenker!"

No one was on the street to hear me, so I listened to my voice echo off the empty glass buildings and parked cars until it was swallowed up by the racing crackle of the city.

I turned left again, into the alley.

It seemed darker than it should have. The moon was out, but there in the alley it was all shadows and half-seen things. I moved cautiously, listening to the crunchy rhythm of my feet on the gravel. Feeling my way through the dark.

Suddenly, my right foot met something firm. Soft but solid. I tried to catch myself, failed, landed hard with my hands on the gravel and my body on something that felt like it didn't belong there.

A man. The kind of man you would expect to see in a dark alley on a cold night. He was in sitting position, his back against a wall with both legs extended forward, sitting like a little kid. The palms of my hands were stinging from the fall. I closed them into fists and pressed myself up until I could stand. I could feel an oozing on my hands. "I'm sorry, I didn't see you," I said.

The man did not stir.

I stood in front of him and let my eyes adjust. He was wearing a pea coat. It looked military, except it was filthy and the left pocket had been torn away. He was passed out cold. Was he dead? I knelt down and put my face close to his. His breath came over me, sour and hot. I gagged. I stood up. A thick, gravelly trail of vomit lay on his coat from chin to belly. His head was cocked to the side, half covered in the thick collar of the jacket. He looked to be fifty. His skin was deeply pocked beneath a thin and strangely well-trimmed beard. Even in the dark, I could see the sores of his heavily chapped lips.

An oily despair flooded through me. I thought to myself, this man is suffering. His is a used-up rag of a life. Who knows what brought him here? Too many bad habits? Terrible luck and dead parents? Perhaps I'm looking at myself a few short years from now? Anything is possible in the frozen-hearted world.

I watched him sleep. I thought, if I were good, I would pick him up, take him to my house, bathe him, and give him my bed to sleep in. That book I used to read tells me this man is none other than Christ himself, waiting for me, waiting for me to help him. But I know what I will do. This world is full of empty gestures.

I continued down the alley. My car was parked there, behind the club. I opened the hatch and pulled out a grey felt blanket that had been in there since last winter. I carried it, clamping it between my arms with my fists pressed together, back to the dark place against the wall. I shook it out and laid it on top of the sleeping homeless soldier. He shifted and grunted and turned his face to the wall. I could see the vomit was frozen.

"Oh man," I said out loud.

I was shivering now. I walked fast back toward the car. I had left the hatch open, so I pulled it shut and kept walking. In a few feet, I reached the end of the alley and turned left once more. The street was well lit, and I saw some people walking back to their cars from the show. I smiled and waved. I was freezing.

One more left turn and I stood in front of the club. My friend was waiting just outside the door.

"You look cold," she said. She handed me a glass. Makers, neat. I took it down in one swallow. It tasted like warmth and civilization.

"Let's go in."

She held the door open for me, and I went back inside and cleared my stuff off the stage and thanked my friends for coming and sold ten CDs and got very drunk.

22. ANGEL'S ENVY

IT WAS A HAPPY TIME. We had been drinking. We were at the bar, sitting in a booth shoulder to shoulder, like little birds on the same branch. We were happy because we had worked a long day and it was joyful work and now the work was done and there was only joy left.

We sipped clean bourbon out of short glass tumblers and the effect was immediate. Your cheeks went red, and your eyes met mine and flashed like flashbulbs, and you reached up and set the overhead lamp to swinging. Light spilled out of the lamp and splashed you with a wild shadow that stumbled over your face and made a sundial of your nose.

"Judging by the looks of things, it's almost midnight," I said.

"My nose," you said, "is telling you the time."

We toasted each other, our glasses touching with a distinctly audible *ting!*

For almost a minute, we did not say anything. I looked at the lamp swinging and then at you with your tumbling shadows and then at the color of the whiskey in the glass, the honey-colored sweetness of it, and then I closed my eyes and listened to the happy buzz of people around us, like bees in honeycomb. I was under the influence of love, and no one around me could do any wrong, and all the buzzing bees were holy pilgrims and children of God, and I was drinking very good whiskey.

"Honey, you are doing that weird thing with your mind, I can tell."

I opened my eyes. You were looking at me, and I could feel your shoulder against my shoulder. The bees disappeared, and it was only you again.

"Oh? What thing is that?"

"That thing where you pay attention to everything at once and then you start thinking about what it all means."

"Does it bother you when I do that?"

"No, except when it makes you unhappy."

"I don't think unhappiness is possible tonight."

Your forehead made three slight wrinkles above the brow. After a moment you said, "I think I have to agree with you. Okay. There is a moratorium on unhappiness. Tonight only."

"Moratorium?" I said, laughing, "When did you start saying *moratorium*?"

"Since I was six."

"You're lying."

"I'm not. I'm very smart. And now I want a cigarette."

We walked out the front door with our glasses to where there was a roped-off section of sidewalk reserved for the purpose. It was much quieter but crowded still. The air was warm with a hint of the cool that means fall has come. It was all part of the happiness. You could see it in the other drinkers. They too felt the cool of the fall and the joy of a perfect southern evening and the dangerous and exhilarating pleasure of drinking with friends and strangers.

I stood beside you and watched you smoke and I listened.

Out of the crowd appeared a man with heavy-rimmed glasses and very short dark hair, asking me for a light. I said, "Sadly, I do not smoke." He agreed that it was sad. But then I said my lovely girl could help, and the right side of his mouth rose up in a half smile. He turned to you, slightly spinning on his heels, and when you lifted your hand to light his cigarette, and the three gold bracelets you wore slid down from the crook of your wrist to settle onto the soft flesh of your forearm, I was grateful to have been blessed with the powers of observation, because the sight was beautiful, and the night grew fatter on its own delight.

The man whose cigarette had just been lit was a stranger, and the expression he wore was a serious one. I was glad he was here because, though we had never spoken, I had seen him many times around town at rock shows and folk shows, often sitting by himself with a concentrated look on his face. If there is any kind of person I like it, is someone who sits by himself.

Just then, a friend of yours appeared whom I did not know. Your eyes widened in surprise and the two of you fell into a bright and busy conversation. The man in front of me leaned back against the rail with the lit cigarette between his thumb and forefinger. He smoked like he was pinching someone.

You were busy talking, and so you did not hear what we said.

"Man, am I glad to see you," I said abruptly. I meant to set a friendly, disarming tone, but the words had no timing about them and they fell from my mouth and landed short.

"I'm sorry. Do I know you?"

"You do. We went to seventh grade together. I sat behind you three rows back in algebra. Remember?" Spinning a farce is a strategy that has worked for me in the past.

I waited while he drew a breath of smoke from his pinched cigarette.

"I don't remember you in algebra. But that girl who lit my cigarette. What's her name?"

I said your name.

He said, "I've seen her play. She's really good."

I agreed. "She is a singular talent. Inspired."

"She's got a lot of stuff going on right now, right?" He named some of the things people knew about: the songs of yours that were recorded by the famous person, the big shows you had recently played.

Then he surprised me.

"I've seen you too. Perform." Then he said my name.

"That is me." I took a slightly nervous sip. "I guess this is that part where I say I was lying a second ago about being in seventh grade algebra with you."

He didn't say anything. He looked at me closely.

Then he said, "My name is Ben. Let's have a serious conversation."

I said I didn't know how to have any other kind. I looked over at you, talking with your girlfriend, laughing at something she said, with your hand draped lazily around the glass.

I looked back at him.

Ben put the cigarette to his lips and drew in a long, slow breath. The orange ball at the tip glowed furiously. He turned his head and exhaled a focused stream of grey smoke and said, "I actually know a thing or two about you. You've been around awhile. You're good. Maybe even very good."

"Maybe," I said.

"You know what you are. What I want to know is, are you jealous?"

"Of what?"

"Of her."

"What do you mean?"

"She's killin' it right now. I haven't really seen your name around lately."

The dark of the night and the heavy framed glasses made it hard to see the shape of his eyes, whether he was to be trusted.

"I got my thing."

He smiled. "I know you do. Forgive me if that was too bold. I'm not very good at making small talk. I was just seeing what you would say."

I suddenly noticed my drink was empty. I told him I would be right back, and I went inside and ordered a new bourbon, Angel's Envy, neat, and I came back out to the smoking porch and he was in the same place in the same posture, waiting for me.

"Well," I said, easing into it, "I'm going to try to answer your question." I took a long sip of the fresh pour. "It's like there are two me's."

"Two me's."

"Yes. One me is jealous—I'll just say it. One me wishes it was me doing all of the cool things. Had the attention, the momentum. That me looks around and says, man I'm great, I've written these songs and have spent a million years working hard at playing guitar and listening to music and being inspired and moving across the country risking everything at all costs for years and years—so why not me?

"But this me—I'm embarrassed to say it but I may as well—is jealous of a lot of things. This me is a towering babel of ego. This is the same me that probably wishes I was the most famous person in the history of the world. Like, more famous than Elvis. In fact, this one time when I was really into making lists, I wrote down a list of names with my name in there so I could look at the kind of company I felt I was worthy of keeping."

"What were the names?"

"Elvis Presley, Michael Jackson, Garth Brooks, and my name."

He laughed, and with the laugh came a little coughing sound.

"Garth Brooks?"

"Garth Brooks sold more records than anyone, ever."

"So you wanted to be one of the greatest selling artists of all time."

"No," I said, "*Want* to be, and not *one* of the greatest selling, *the* greatest selling. Well, maybe not the greatest selling, just the most influential. You know, posters of my album cover in Times Square, ten times on the cover of *Rolling Stone*, my own TV show, which would become so successful that I would acquire my own communications company, which I would name after myself and gradually get bigger and bigger until I owned some island nation in the South Pacific or something. This me wants to be King of the World."

"So you want to be, like, a male Oprah?"

"Yeah, except Oprah can't play guitar, so I would have that on her."

The little laughing cough came again.

"So this me of yours, this me is jealous."

"Obviously."

He looked me in the eye and nodded his head slowly up and down.

I thought he was going to ask me about the other me, which was a pretty good story, but instead he lifted his shoe and stubbed the cigarette out on the sole. Then, very methodically, he withdrew a new pack of Parliaments from his jacket pocket, gave it one short, focused shake, and took the clean white cigarette that poked out from the pack and put it to his lips. In the same slight spinning motion he had done earlier, he turned and asked you for another light. You paused in your own conversation to hand him your lighter, which is when he said, "Your boyfriend is an egomaniac, to put it lightly."

"He has some redeeming qualities," you answered. Our eyes met, laughing.

He used his thumb to flick the lighter to life. He passed the lighter back to you and said, "But I'm about to hear the rest of the story."

You took the lighter from him and said, "It's probably a good story." You true heart.

Ben turned once more to me and said, "So, to recap, one me—the me we've heard from so far—is jealous of your famous girlfriend because you are jealous of anyone who is in any way more successful than you. Or younger, or more beautiful, or a better guitar player, or whatever."

"That's pretty much it. This me—maybe we'll call him Normal Me—wishes I was universally recognized as being the most amazing person of all time. Anything short of that is a disappointment."

"Sounds pretty painful."

"It's more than painful. It's ridiculous. And were it not for the other me, there's no way I could hang out with her (I raised my glass in your direction), because she would feel my jealousy and she would have to get away from me. She's delicate that way. Negative feelings affect her more than anyone else I know."

He smiled. "She is a much better person than you."

"She is a much better person than most people."

The orange ball glowed and grew dim.

"So what about the other me? And no bullshit."

I took a sip from the honeyed bourbon in my glass, which in the dim light of the smoking porch had assumed the color of maple syrup. I took a deep breath. I felt afraid.

"I don't know how else to say this. But the other me is barely there."

"Barely there."

"Yes, barely there. The other me is, like, a . . . not-me. An anti-me."

"Sounds Buddhist," said Ben. "Sounds fruity."

I laughed when he said that, because fruity is one of my favorite words. I hate fruity things.

"It is sort of Buddhist, I guess," I said, pausing to take the sip. I held the whiskey in my mouth for several seconds and swallowed. "As far as Buddhism is concerned with the destruction of the self, I guess I am Buddhist. But those are just words—destruction of the self—and, most of the time, words are bullshit. Words are very confusing things."

"That much is true." We toasted.

It was hard to see what Ben looked like, I noticed. The frames on his glasses were so heavy they absorbed all your attention. A wall of thick glass.

"Anyway," I said, "There is a much more direct path, and that's the one I try to follow."

Ben said: "You are going to tell me you are a Christian, and that your faith in God is what keeps you from being an asshole."

"No, I think a lot of times I'm still an asshole. Normal Me has been around for a long time and doesn't want to check out of the hotel just yet." To myself I thought, maybe I should have put some ice in this bourbon.

"But your thing is a Christian thing."

I could tell where this was going and it was painful. I said a quick prayer that I might find the words, the right words.

"I don't know how to say this without using words you've heard a million times. Empty words. Bumper sticker words. I don't ever talk about this stuff directly. I don't know how. The words have been used and overused and misshapen by selfish people and basically hammered into whatever crude meaning for so long that they've lost their sparkle. I need new words and I don't have them."

Ben was still interested, as evidenced in the way he

was listening. He was looking at me the way I had seen him look at the artists at rock clubs. He was watching the show.

"Well," he said, "You might as well try to explain yourself. In the words you have."

I looked into my glass. I didn't want to say anything more, because I was going to have to use the words. And the words would make a wall more perfect than Ben's glasses. He had heard them all before. Words can die out in the desert, all alone, and never live again, if you're not careful.

Still, this was a moment. And you have to try to meet your moment.

"Okay. Basically, Ben, I am a sinner. My default way of going about the challenge of life is to put myself first in every and all situations, which eventually and inevitably leads to ruin. Mine and other people's. I know this because I am well practiced in the art of selfish living. I am probably the most selfish person I know."

"You probably are," said Ben, shifting his weight.

I laughed. Ben was good company. "Anyway, do you really want to hear this? Living my life in pursuit of my own happiness has only made me unhappy. *I can't ever get there, stay there, have it, keep it.* It seems like it's that way for everyone. It's a sad story, and you can watch it play out in a million variations in the lives of everyone around you. People get what they think they want and then they spent the rest of their lives afraid they might lose it. Or people don't get what they think they want and they hate everyone else who does. Misery. A loud wailing chorus of worldwide misery."

"Depressing." Ben had finished his cigarette and was now once more leaning back against the railing of the smoking area. Behind him on the boulevard, a police car sped past with its lights on but no siren.

"Damn depressing," I said. "So the only solution, really, the only thing to do, is just give up. Everything. All of it. All the time. Walk around giving up. Wake up giving up. It sort of sucks because it's really hard to do, and unless you're Ghandi or some boring person who wasn't very selfish in the first place, you find you are always trying to take it back. Normal Self really wants the ball. So you just walk around giving up the ball and then picking it back up and fucking up and then remembering what it's all about and giving it up again. That's pretty much my life right now."

Ben reached out and took my drink out of my hand, took a sip, and handed it back to me. "I'm not sure it's much of an improvement."

"You might be right. I'm sort of making it up as I go along."

For about four seconds, Ben watched me like he was checking me for flaws. Then he pressed his lips together like he had decided something. He turned to you and said, "You two are an interesting duo. I'll see you around." And you stopped talking to that girl long enough to shake his hand and you said, "It was very nice to meet you." He said his name and you said yours.

After Ben left, we stood for a while longer on the smoking porch with the other happy drinkers. I watched you talk to your friend, and I took another sip of bourbon from the glass. I held it in my mouth, tasting the sweetness of it, and the heat.

23. NEW YEAR'S DAY AND THE GREAT SNAKE

LET EVERYONE ELSE TELL you their resolutions. I'm telling you a story.

Two days ago, I woke up in the town where I was raised: Twin Falls, Idaho. It was snowing. Great big complicated flakes that fell without noise or fuss. Wet snow. Good snow. It had been awhile, so I decided to go for a walk.

I put on my little brother's boots and my dad's good hat and set out. There were crunching sounds, and I could see my breath. I was happy.

I don't know why, but in my pocket I brought with me a short stack of 3 × 5 cards. I have a habit when I'm reading of writing down quotes I like. And I keep these in a stack on my dresser. Sometimes, at odd moments, I sit down and read them.

Anyway, I brought some from Nashville for the trip home. Just a random collection pinched off the top of the stack. Maybe twenty cards. It had been a long time since I had looked at any of them. So here I am, walking down the street I grew up on, pulling a card out of my pocket and reading it.

We have now sunk to a depth at which the restatement of the obvious is the first duty of intelligent men.
—George Orwell

I laughed. My breath squirted out of me and made little shapes in the cold air. That was probably something I had written down a long time ago. I remembered I used to enjoy pithy words like this because they led me to believe there were people out there—like George Orwell, I guess—who were in possession of forgotten knowledge and who could be counted on to come forward and set the rest of us straight. I also remembered once driving past a billboard for a church that said simply in white letters on black, "We know the way!" and I thought, "Man, I should go to that church." I am a sucker for confident statements.

There were no cars, so I walked down the middle of the street. The snow still falling and crunching. The day cold and grey and bright and me warm in my own pea coat and my dad's good hat. I dug into my pocket for another card.

Search your own heart with all diligence for out of it flow all the issues of life.
—Proverbs 4:23

Well, I thought, I don't remember when I wrote this down, but it still means something to me. I looked at it and read it again out loud. "Search your own heart with all diligence for out it flow all the issues of life." The quiet snow made the words sound holy. I thought, "I love this because I feel it is true. And my own experience confirms it. I have never failed when I've listened to my heart without bias or predisposition."

Then, I thought, "I am the most religious agnostic person I know." I laughed. More breathy shapes in the air.

The road I was on turned into another, and so I headed right, toward the river. The river was the Snake—a slow old man who lives in the bottom of the canyon with his enormous sturgeon fish and a lot of my childhood memories. I walked and thought about how I had almost drowned on my seventeenth birthday because I tried to swim below the Shoshone Falls, just upriver from here. But how I had loved almost drowning because the girl I was dating at the time was there to watch and worry over me. Ah, a boy will subject himself to any number of horrors as long as there's a girl there to cry over him. "Man, I should write that down," I thought.

Another random card.

Perhaps it will turn out that you are called to be an artist. Then take that destiny upon yourself and bear it, its burden and its greatness, without ever asking what recompense might come from outside.
—Rainer Maria Rilke

That one is a secret. You can't publicly identify with statements that include the words "burden," "artist," and "greatness" because you sound like a pompous ass. Especially when you are poor and unknown. Because then you are in danger of being proud of your poorness and your unknown-ness, and nothing is more stupid than that. I dropped the card in the snow and kept walking, which didn't matter, because I had read it so many times I couldn't forget it if I tried.

I was a few miles away from home now and the wind was picking up. I was still warm, and there were several cards to read and thoughts to think, so I pressed on and after another quiet mile, I was standing on the jagged lip of the Snake River Canyon. If only you could have seen this magnificent thing. Five hundred feet deep and nearly straight down all the way. Black, wet rock carelessly decorated with white snow, and in the bottom a lazy blue river that had been there since the beginning of time. Idaho is a magical place. A card:

It's no good trying to get rid of your own aloneness. You've got to stick to it all your life. Only at times, at times, the gap will be filled in. At times! But you have to wait for the times.
Accept your own aloneness and stick to it, all your life. And then accept the times when the gap is filled in, when they come.
But they've got to come. You can't force them.
—D.H. Lawrence

I put the card back in my pocket and looked out on my childhood canyon and the great void before me. I stood for a long time. And then I sat. I felt the cold snow on my butt and the cold wind on my face and looked at the bluing twilight sky and I thought how very lucky I was to be alive. To feel cold and warm, to be inspired and disillusioned, to bleed and be healed, to see my laugh poke out and dissolve in the air before me, to feel lonely and loved. It was so good. This life.

Just then, a gust of wind took the hat off my head and carried it over the lip of the canyon. "Oh shit!" I yelled and stood up and made some kind of vague gesture of saving it. But no. I watched it tumble down and down and then disappear into the milky blue river. "Oh shit," I said again. That was my dad's good hat. And I am a broke-ass clown poet.

I turned around and walked away from the gaping canyon and began conjuring the funny story I would tell my father about how the dogs up the street had tackled me and stolen his hat right off my head and how lucky I was to be alive.

It would be funny when I told it. Then I would ask my mom where he got it, and then I would spend some time on Ebay.

24. SUPERMAN AND LOIS LANE

AT LAST, I CAN'T STAND IT.

"My virtue is so boring!" I shout, and slam my fist onto the desk with a thud that makes the pencils rattle in their holder. But then I remember my sleeping roommate, and a guilt borne by habit slumps my shoulders. I am still again.

Staring out the window of my bedroom—which triples as my office and recording studio—I look like a serious person. The blue morning light falls sideways through the curtain and lands on my face at an odd angle, exaggerating my large nose and boney forehead. I am not ugly, but my features have a certain cartoonish hue about them, as though I was a caricature of myself. To my right, a particleboard bookshelf bearing a weathered rainbow of paperbacks—mostly novels by dead people—looks on, completing the scene.

Seeing this cartoon-man scowling intensely out the window, you will guess I am thinking carefully. I am not. Careful thinking is precise, orderly, and this is something more like intellectual flailing. Two dozen ideas clamor for attention like kindergarten children all raising their hands at once. It is noisy.

I should write a book about spiritual depravity in
modern life.
That girl at the coffee shop is hot.
Is it too early to watch *30 Rock* on Hulu?
I haven't written a good song in three months.
I need to recycle more.
Maybe I should buy a handgun; that would be unpredictable.
Oh, that Pro Tools quick key is going to come in handy!
Why am I so concerned about being unpredictable?
My songs are all out of touch.
I wish Fluevog would make a shoe and call it the Korby.
Shit, I have to text that dude.
My dad's birthday was last week. I am a bad son.
The rain forests of South America.
At what point has a person officially squandered his potential?
The only thing left that's good about me is that I don't care what
anyone thinks.
That's a lie. I care what everyone thinks.
I have got to stop drinking coffee.
My roommate is a total asshole.

I need to buy more underwear.

What is wrong with me?

What's wrong with me is I'm thirty-three years old and I can't pay my rent again. Despite all my efforts, I don't understand anything nor can I even begin to make sense of it. Church depresses me. Books make me crazy. Music makes me want to take drugs. My culture's obsession with TV and movies and pop everything is making me seriously consider ending my participation in the whole enterprise. The only thing I've got is my ridiculous sense of dignity, which makes me appear to be happy and even mischievous to everyone around me, when in fact I am being forcibly crushed by the impossible obligation of staying alive without constantly lying to myself. I hate liars. I also hate pussies. I also hate the word pussy, which I never would have used ten years ago, another example of how far I've slipped from the good-natured idealism of my youth.

And so on. I am rolling. Seven thirty in the morning and already drunk on the high of my own self-loathing. Please don't feel sorry for me. Secretly, I am enjoying myself. Mine is a delight not unlike that of a man being slapped in the face mid-thrust by the lover astride him. The sting makes the pleasure bite, makes it stick. The trick is to keep the self-awareness just off camera, so I can believe what I am saying.

At the door, then, a knock. My roommate's head appears. The head says, "Dude, the rent. I need it, man."

What I want to say is, "Dude, I'll give you the fucking rent when you pick up your shit. Maybe clean that skyscraper of dishes in the sink. Or the forest of pubes on the toilet; I mean, you could knit a sock. Maybe if you didn't utterly disregard every normal standard of human consideration, I'd be more inclined to participate in the financial well-being of this household. I've asked you nicely, like, six times. Clearly, you don't give a shit. So I'm forced to do the only thing I can do, which is say fuck you to the rent until you nut up and clean your filth."

What I actually say is, "Um, yeah. The rent. Cool. I'll write you a check. Hey, could you maybe try to wash those dishes in the sink?"

"Oh yeah, totally. Man, I'm sorry, I don't know what my problem is. I get so caught up in my drama . . . you know, Claire and all that."

Claire is my roommate's girlfriend, or arch-nemesis, depending on which day of the week it is. When I first met him, he had a black eye, because they had gotten in an argument the night before and Claire had punched him in the face. I moved in two days later, because I am a genius.

"Right," I say, fumbling through the drawer of my desk to find the checkbook.

He stays on and watches me. "Man, did we wake you up last night?"

I stop searching and look at him blankly.

"Shit. Sorry," he says. "I thought it would be fun

to light some bottle rockets, you know, Labor Day and all."

"Dude, those were my bottle rockets. It was four in the morning."

"Yeah, but you said they were for everybody. And I dunno, I thought if I shot 'em far enough they wouldn't really make much noise."

This makes sense to my roommate. He is one of those people for whom the world exists only as a backdrop for his own personal adventure. The rest of us live outside the membrane, which protects everything within and distorts and distances everything without.

"Ah, life inside the membrane. Must be warm in there," I say.

He laughs lightheartedly. "Man, am I hung over. I was so wasted last night."

At last, the checkbook. It is Superman themed. There are four in the series, and the one on top shows Superman holding Lois Lane in his arms. I turn the page. That one is only for handing to girls. But, oh good, the next is classic: Superman sticking out his chest with his head turned slightly to the right. I write the amount in the box and hand it to the dude, who says, "Cool! See you later. Me and Claire are goin' to Knoxville for the weekend. Her cousin's getting married. We got a rental car and everything!"

He shuts my door. I listen to his heavy footsteps make their way through the apartment. The loud slam of the front door. A few seconds later, the sound of a car leaving the gravel parking lot and then a silver Nissan Sentra moving pluckily across the street, left to right. He turns to me and waves.

I sit back in my chair and look up at the ceiling and wonder where am I going to get the three hundred bucks I need to cover the rent. Figure I have two days before it clears. I look down at the checkbook. Back on top is the one I like, Superman and Lois Lane.

25. PAGE OF SWORDS

LOOK AT ME SITTING THERE, slouching deep into a leather overstuffed chair, my shoulders pressed up and in so that I look like I have no neck. You can tell I am nervous because I keep shifting the position of my arms. For a while they are folded in my lap, now they're resting on the arms of the chair, godfather-like. I am trying to look comfortable. The wall behind me is made entirely of glass, and even though it is an overcast day with rain streaking down the windows, the light is still tremendous. Cold and bright.

Across the room, leaning against the kitchen counter, my friend is telling me about bamboo. His name is Jack, and he is telling me about bamboo because that's what his floor is made of. We are in his apartment, and it is a fancy apartment, six stories up in a part of town called the Gulch, which is a fancy part of town. His floor is made of bamboo, he is saying, which is nice because it's softer than other wood floors.

I look down at the floor. Yellow. It is hard to tell how soft it is, but it's a beautiful floor.

"It's a beautiful floor," I say.

He doesn't acknowledge the compliment. He has more to tell me about bamboo, how it only blooms once every hundred years, and when it blooms, it blooms everywhere, all the bamboo.

"Everywhere in the world, all at once."

I think he is probably exaggerating, but he is one of those people you just kind of believe. He has a way of saying things that makes them true even when they aren't.

While he talks, I look past him into the kitchen, which is part of the living room, in the modern style. The kitchen is immaculately clean, but there are a few appliances on the counter so as to suggest occasional use.

I know, because once, several months ago, he made me a dinner of stir fry, and I sat on one of his barstools and ate it with chopsticks. I didn't know him very well then and was suspicious he had an agenda, so between bites of water chestnuts and snap peas I asked him if he was gay. He told me matter-of-factly that he was not.

"Men are dirty and crude and simple. I put up with men. Women, I like. Hot, complicated, difficult women."

"So shouldn't you be making dinner for a hot, complicated woman tonight?" I asked.

"I made dinner for her last night. Tonight is bro night."

Bro night ended in singular fashion. Let me tell you, so you understand the kind of person we are talking about. After the stir fry dinner, we went to Jack's friend's house. The friend was having a big party with couples making out on the front porch and a big fire in the backyard. I met a few people I didn't like, and toward the end of the evening, about a dozen of us were standing around the fire drinking Bulleit whiskey from the bottle. The bottle went around a few times, and suddenly Jack pulled a roll of five dollar bills out of his pocket and handed them to everyone who was there. Everyone got two and some people got three. Then Jack made a speech about how people need to free themselves from the corrupting power of money, how America's obsession with money was going to be the end of everything good in the world. He even quoted a Bible verse. Then he threw his money into the fire. He had a handful of fives, and when they hit the flames they burned slowly, catching orange at the corners and withering inward to an ashy black. He nudged me with his elbow, so I threw my two fives in, one after the other. It felt very strange. It felt wrong, actually. Then everyone else threw their money in, and some of them started cheering, and then there was this sense of euphoria around the fire. We all looked each other in the eyes and smiled, and one couple started making out; Jack had to steer them away from the flames because they were drunk and losing their balance. We burned about three hundred dollars in less than a minute. That was Jack's version of generosity.

A fine memory, but here I am now, sinking into Jack's expensive leather chair on a rainy November day, wondering what we are going to do, why he asked me to come over.

He is done with his soliloquy on bamboo and is now pouring scotch into a pair of tumblers. He walks across the room, and the sound of his wooden-soled shoes against the wooden floor is pleasant. Fatherly. He hands me a glass.

"Simon," he says, "How are things with you?"

This is odd, because he never asks me about me, which is one of the things I like about him.

"Never better," I say, taking a sip.

"You're probably lying, but I'll get to that in a moment. I need to ask you a favor."

"Okay?"

"I need you to walk with me to the McDonald's to return this movie." He holds out a Redbox DVD case.

I am surprised and I laugh out loud. "Um, okay. What movie is it?"

"It's not important, but I would like for you to come with me to take it back."

"Sure, man. But what movie is it? I'm curious what Jack Needham rents from a Redbox."

"You may die wondering. Let me get my coat."

We take the elevator downstairs and walk out the front door of the building into the grey, rainy day.

We walk in silence for a few blocks. It's Sunday and there aren't very many people out. We walk past a restaurant with outdoor seating, but all the metal chairs are pulled into the tables, and there is a cable running through the legs of the chairs, chaining them together.

"Patio convicts," I say to myself.

"What?'

"Um, nothing. It didn't really make sense."

Jack turns to me. "Man, you have got to stop mumbling. That's one thing."

"What do you mean, *one thing*? Are there several things?"

Jack doesn't respond.

The rain is coming down lightly, but otherwise it's warm outside. I am starting to sweat inside my coat.

We come upon an Urban Outfitters, and just as we pass, a pretty girl comes out of the front door and sees Jack and smiles. She doesn't look at me.

"Annoying." I say it loud enough so Jack can hear.

"She'd look at you too if you demanded it," he says, eyes forward.

"How do you know it's the girl I'm annoyed about?"

"Men are crude and simple, Simon."

The avenue bends left and we start walking uphill. Rain. Sweat. Why are we going to a McDonald's? It is unlike him. I didn't think Jack watched movies. He's too busy planning expeditions to climb mountains in the Andes (true story) to fuss with pop culture. But then, men are crude and simple. I wonder what movie.

We arrive at the intersection of 12th and Division. We are waiting for the light. There's a topless bar across the street. While we wait, I watch the neon sign flicker on and off. Showgirls. One hundred pretty girls and three ugly ones, the sign says.

"Great lunch buffet there," Jack says, pointing.

I feel sticky under my coat and it's starting to rain harder.

"Jack," I say. "What are we doing?" I have to shout because the traffic is heavy and fast.

"You'll see."

The light changes and we cross the street. Jack walks slightly ahead of me. I can see the McDonald's.

It's dinner time, so there are a lot of cars in the drive-thru lane. We pass the front door and round the corner where the machine is. A line has queued up in front of the Redbox machine. There are two people in front of us. Jack is calm.

"Did you know McDonald's opens a new restaurant every four hours?" Jack says to me. "Every four hours. Insane."

The first person has finished and now the second person is at the screen, a skinny bald man with Lennon-style glasses and blue sweats. His drooping pointer finger jabs at the screen a dozen times. He is taking forever.

Finally, he's done. Jack efficiently, familiarly, pushes the buttons on the screen. The Redbox makes a whirring sound and the DVD case disappears inside.

Jack turns to me and says, "Thanks. Now, there's someone I want you to meet."

He turns and walks through the door of the McDonald's. I follow. Nothing surprises me.

The restaurant is busy. The lights are bright and white and it is loud inside and there are a lot of people. Kids. Some of them are crying. I look behind the counter and people are yelling at each other. Not angry, just yelling. It is a McDonald's at dinnertime in America.

Jack keeps walking, back toward the bathrooms. At the last booth, he stops. There is an enormous black lady sitting in the booth by herself, facing the door, facing me. You can tell she has been there a long time because there's a tray on the table, and on the tray are six or seven hamburger wrappers stained with ketchup. She looks at me and sniffs.

"Simon." Jack smiles. "This is Shawna. She's a fortune teller."

"Bullshit," I say, laughing, cautious.

Shawna looks at Jack and says, "Well, fuck this little cracker. I don't give a shit."

Jack scowls at me, sits down next to the lady. He can only sit half on the bench, because she is taking up the rest of it. He puts his arm around her and gestures at me. "Shawna, honey, he's just stiff — I mean, look at him; he's scared to death. I've told him all about you, and he really wants to have his fortune told."

She looks at me skeptically. "He got money?"

"He'll pay whatever he needs to." He looks at me and winks.

She shrugs her shoulders. "Sit down, skinny man."

The look on Jack's face lets me know he's having the time of his life. He stands up and takes the tray with all the hamburger wrappers away. I sit down, facing Madame Shawna. Now that I'm looking, I can see how alert her expression is. She is looking straight at me. She holds out her hands face up.

"Put your hands on mine," she says.

I do. Her hands are filmy and gross. I don't want her to touch me. But she closes her fingers around mine and shuts her eyes. Her hair is very short and black except for a patch above her right ear, which is earl grey. Her hands twitch once while she holds mine. I don't say anything.

Jack comes back and is now sitting in the booth across the aisle, watching us. He has a Cheshire grin on his face.

Shawna opens her eyes and releases my hands. I want to go wash them. I'm perspiring heavily beneath my coat. My attention turns to the bead of sweat dripping from my armpit, cooling as it falls.

Then Shawna reaches into her purse, which is lying beside her in the booth. She pulls out an enormous deck of tarot cards. It is the first time I have ever seen a pack of tarot cards.

"You seen these before, chicken?"

I assume by chicken she means me. "No, only read about them."

She clucks her tongue. "Tarot cannot be read about. Only *experienced.*"

I look over at Jack, now positively shaking with excitement in the booth beside ours. I have never seen him so happy, not even when he made us burn the money.

While Shawna spreads the cards out on the table, a Hispanic man carrying a child passes us on the way to the bathroom. He sees what is going on. He looks suspicious. I don't blame him.

Shawna shuffles the cards, and while she does, I notice how worn they are. That gives me some confidence. You don't want to see a brand new pack of tarot cards when you're having your fortune told at a McDonald's. She hands them to me to shuffle. I have a hard time of it, because the cards are huge and my fingers and small and bad with details.

I cut the deck into four piles, and she lays them out in the shape a half-moon. Some of the cards are vertical, and some of them are horizontal. All of them are face down. She places both hands flat on the table, takes a deep breath, and begins turning them over.

Knight of Wands
Five of Swords
Seven of Cups
Queen of Pentacles
Knight of Cups
King of Pentacles

Page of Swords
Six of Cups
Eight of Cups
Six of Pentacles

She looks the cards over for a long time. I gesture to Jack, and he hands me a pen. I write down the names of all the cards she flipped so I can look them up later. A feeling of keen curiosity takes hold. I am having my fortune told at the McDonald's on Broadway. Jack tricked me.

Finally, Madame Shawna is done looking at the cards. She takes a deep breath. "This is a very special situation, young man. You are in store for a great adventure."

I'm not going to tell you the details. You know the cards. You can look them up yourself.

26. TWO RED RINGS

"**MOM, YOU HAVE TO** let it go. I'm not going to grad school. Or med school. Or law school. I'm going to be poor and dumb for the rest of my life."

"Oh, Korby. You don't have to put it like that. I'm just saying, you have such a mind, you could be anything you want to be."

The phone is getting heavy in my hand.

"I know I can be anything I want to be, and I'm being it, Mom. If you liked music, you would understand that."

"Oh, Korby. We like music. It's just that everything has its place. Music has its place. But so does a career. So does family. Music doesn't pay the bills. You have to be realistic."

"I don't know what realistic means. And I pay my bills just fine."

"But not with your music! Korby, you're a *car parker!*"

"A valet, Mom. And a really good one. Probably one of the best. Plus, I look great in my uniform."

"Korby, anyone can park cars. *Criminals* can park cars!"

"No they can't, Mom. They do a license check on that sort of thing. Besides, you should see me drive. I'm super good at it. People stand and applaud when I pull their car up to the curb. They shake my hand. They give me hundred-dollar bills. They offer me their daughters."

"Stop joking, Korby! You're a college graduate! You're not sixteen anymore! This is real life!"

You can hear the frustrated tears in her voice. The thing is, I know she means well.

"Mom, if you wanted to make me feel bad, it's working. I don't really know what to say. I'm not going to stop doing this. I know you don't understand, but I'm really good at what I do. Just because I'm not rich or on TV doesn't mean I suck."

"Korby, no one is saying you suck."

It's funny to hear my mom say suck. It sounds dirty coming out of her mouth.

"Okay. Not suck. But you think I'm wasting my life."

Silence.

"Exactly," I say. "But I don't think I'm wasting my life. I think I'm doing what I should be doing. I make people feel things."

"Oh, Korby, I don't know. We just want you to be happy. What if you get sick? What if you get cancer? We won't be able to help you."

"Mom, I promise not to get cancer until I get a job that has health insurance. Okay?"

I hear her reluctant smile. "We just worry about you so much. Tennessee isn't like Idaho. You're so far away."

I wonder what she means by that, but I don't ask. "I'm okay, Mom. It's okay."

I ask her about Dad, what they've been up to lately. The subject change works wonders on our conversation. She grows animated again. Telling me about the new driveway being poured. What's going on at church. How much weight she's lost since she started speed-walking. It's nice to hear her happy.

I send my love to Dad and we hang up and I'm alone again, driving down I-75 from Knoxville to Atlanta.

The CD player is trying to play the Avett Brothers record I just bought, but I can't really hear it because the old Volvo makes a lot of its own music at this speed. A loud hum, mostly.

For fun, I find the pitch and match it with my own hum. I vary the pitch slightly and listen to the weird dissonant sound it makes as my hum wobbles in and out of tune with the car's.

Through the windshield, I can see the grey sky is starting to crack in places, showing bits of yellow and orange, like the last leaves hanging on before the dark November night takes over. To my left and right, the brown, leafless trees look huddled and annoyed. Like it all ended too soon. Every year, it surprises me how different the world looks without leaves. Prickly.

It's only three in the afternoon, but already there's a long string of headlights in the northbound lane. The Avett Brothers are singing about Brooklyn. I can sort of hear it over the whine and the hum and the brown branches.

Suddenly, I remember. I should tweet about my show tonight at Eddie's Attic. I know a few people in Decatur. Some of them will come.

I am typing what I think is a funny tweet about my show. It's difficult because the iPhone keypad is small and I have never gotten used to it, not even if I turn it sideways. Plus, I am driving.

I must be pretty proud of myself, because I'm laughing while I type. This is going to be good. Everyone who lives within a hundred miles of Atlanta is going to come to my show tonight because I am so witty.

I push send, but suddenly something is wrong. There are new lights. Not in the northbound lane. I look in the rearview mirror, where the lights are coming from. They are right behind me, attached to the top of a state patrol car. They are flashing.

"Oh shit" is what I say. I am not always witty.

While I'm pulling over, I take stock in my situation and realize this is going to be potentially disastrous. For one, sound check at Eddie's is at 6 P.M., ninety minutes from now. For two, on my passenger seat is something that should not be there. Not in plain sight, at least.

I look over, and there it is in plain sight. "Hide!" I shout.

People in desperate circumstances do comical things. Imagine a person who, while trying to look as though he is sitting straight from the shoulders up, is bending his arm in an unnatural way, reaching over to the passenger seat in an unlikely attempt to toss a joint where? Under the seat, I guess? What do people do in this situation? Maybe I should go to grad school.

I fling the thing under the passenger seat, or try to. I can't really tell if I am successful, because I'm slowing down, pulling over, trying to sit up straight, and trying to be clever all at the same time. The humming of the Volvo gets quieter, the Avett Brothers get louder. I turn the brothers down. My hands start shaking.

At moments like these, quotations from books I've read sometimes force their way into my head. I had read something the night before in a Dostoyevsky novel called *The Idiot*, but before I can remember it, a uniform walks up to the passenger side of my idling car. I roll down the window. This can go one of two ways.

"Did you know you were doin' eighty-five back there?"

This is shocking to me. "Well, to be honest, I didn't think this car went that fast, officer. It's an old car."

I think he is looking at me but maybe not. It's hard to tell with the sunglasses. The southern accent is thick. Those glasses are cool, though.

"Okay," he says.

I am sitting on my hands, and I watch in the mirror

as he walks around the back of the car and comes to the driver's side door.

"Could you step out of the car for me and walk back here? I need to ask you a few questions. Go ahead and cut the engine off." His name tag says Milton.

He opens the door, and I follow him to the little space between the back of my old grey station wagon and his brand new cop car. The lights are flashing. They are not blue and red, just white.

"Okay, now stand with your feet apart, like this," he says from behind.

I don't like what I think is about to happen.

He pulls one of my arms behind my back and then the other one. He holds my wrists with one hand while the other pats down first the front of my legs, then the back.

This is what happens right before someone gets handcuffed, I think to myself.

On cue, I hear a sound like the ratchet in a socket set, which, of course, isn't a ratchet at all. It's the first handcuff sliding around my left wrist.

As he cinches the other cuff painfully tight on my right wrist, I remember the quote from last night:

HE BELONGED TO the category of unquestionably intelligent persons who spend their whole lives behaving idiotically.

"That pretty much says it," I say out loud.

"What was that?" asks the cop.

"Um, well, I guess I should ask what this is all about," I say, playing out the farce just a little bit longer.

"I'll show you."

He walks up to the passenger side of my car, opens the door, and removes a nicely rolled joint from the floorboard of the car.

I shrug my shoulders and give him my best Ferris Bueller smile. I am actually relieved, because now I don't have to lie. I hate liars. Plus, whatever happens from here on out, at least it'll be interesting.

He leads me to his patrol car. My arms are locked behind me. It is remarkably uncomfortable.

While we walk, I think, "Wow, I am that guy you see on the side of the road being arrested. How strange. People will wonder what I did."

Just then a blue Tercel drives past with a University of Tennessee sticker on the bumper and two young girls inside, their pretty faces watching me in mild amusement through the window.

Officer Milton opens the door to the back seat. I was right. This is interesting.

"Watch your head," he says, not unkindly.

Then I am inside. The cream-colored vinyl makes a rubbery sound when I sit down on it, and my feet have to bend sideways to fit between the seat and the plexiglass wall.

"Not a lot of leg room, is there?" I say.

Officer Milton doesn't quite smile, but he is not

being meaner than the law mandates, either. He is not a bad guy, I can tell. I can also tell he can tell I'm not a bad guy. We understand each other. Whatever happens, it's going to happen between two gentlemen.

"It's supposed to be uncomfortable. Now, I'm going to search your car. Sit tight."

"I'll be right here."

I watch as he pulls everything out of my car. Two guitar cases, the amp, suitcase. CDs, blankets, whatever he can find. He is opening the guitar cases, and I admire his thoroughness, but then I am distracted by a more pressing concern.

Yes, it is uncomfortable sitting in the back seat of a patrol car with your hands pinned behind you in tight handcuffs. It's really uncomfortable. My wrists feel like they're being bent backward by a pair of giant pliers. Part of the genius of handcuffs is that they make your elbows and shoulders ache too, more than you'd think. But what grabs my attention now is worse than all that: there is a mosquito—one dying November mosquito—buzzing around the back of the patrol car. And I am locked inside with no escape.

The mosquito is humming around my head. In the quiet of this sealed-up car, the sound is total, obnoxious. I try to bonk it with my head by jerking suddenly to the left. It doesn't work. The mosquito settles on my right thigh. I make a violent shifting motion and it compels him to fly over to my left. Another shift and we are in full battle, only I am at a severe disadvantage. I slide back and forth on the back seat. This is insulting.

"If I didn't have these handcuffs, I would end you so fast," I say through bared teeth. The mosquito answers by landing on the side of my neck. I try to move but I can't, because for the moment I am a restrained criminal. I can actually hear the blood being sucked out of my body. I slump my shoulders.

"This is insulting."

At last, the gentleman officer has finished putting everything back in my car. He opens his own door and sits inside, writing on some paper.

"Are you comfortable?" he asks.

"There's a mosquito back here and he just got me."

The officer chuckles. I frown, because I wasn't actually trying to be funny that time.

He says, "So, you play music?"

"With all my heart." I say it kind of mockingly, kind of not. I can tell he gets it.

"I play guitar, too. What was that in the case there? A Martin?"

"Yeah, a D-18. I bought it new."

"You put all those scratches in it?"

"I'm trying to give Willie Nelson a run for his money."

"You might make it, kid. You might just make it."

He gets out of the driver's seat, comes around to my door, and opens it. Grabs me by the arm, not roughly. Helps me out.

The traffic is flying by. Headlights and taillights and

everything loud and fast. It is the greyest twilight ever invented.

"Now, I'm going to let you out of these things," he says loudly over the traffic. "Don't do something that would make me mad."

"Okay" seems to be the right reply.

When the second handcuff comes off, I swear a handful of starlings shoot out of the prickly trees above and fly over the freeway.

I turn around and face my arrestor.

He says, "Here is a ticket. I'm taking this CD of yours." It's a copy of *King of Hearts*. "I hope I didn't make you late for your gig."

"Cool, man," I say. "It's yours."

While we shake hands, I think, Too bad there wasn't a film crew, this could have been on *COPS*. At least an outtake or something. Maybe, like, the touching holiday episode.

I jump in the car and drive fast but not too fast and make it to Eddie's Attic in time for my set and wonder if anyone notices the two bright red rings around my wrists. A couple of times, I almost say something, but then I think that would be a bad idea. I should probably wait and write about it later.

27. SIMON CICADA

FROM THE OUTSIDE, Simon Cicada was just like any other nymph. He drank a lot of root juice, he was good at digging tunnels, he had perfect pitch. His exoskeleton was flawless but for a chip just to the right of his jaw, testament to a botched attempt to chew through what he thought was an acorn but turned out to be a rock.

He wasn't one of the smartest bugs in the brood. That much he knew. When he dropped from the Big Tree so many years ago, it took more than a few hours to figure out what to do next. One second he was lying in the grass with his fifty squishy siblings, and the next everyone was gone. Simon still couldn't recall the memory without shuddering. There he was, a helpless newborn, alone in the big, bright world, soft-skinned and juicy. It was a miracle a bird hadn't eaten him. He thought he was left for dead until his brother Zeke poked his head up and suggested he join everyone at their new home underground. Simon was a slow learner.

But the years since had not been unkind. What he lacked in good sense he made up in enthusiasm. He won a few underground contests, mostly for digging but once for singing. He had a few friends. He knew a cool trick he could do with his middle eye that made the girls giggle. It was alright, and alright was pretty good for a cicada.

In time, he found he had a natural knack with languages, having picked up Beetlese almost immediately, and later Worm. For awhile, he ran the Worm Communications Department and was in charge of all diplomatic relations between his species and theirs. And while he enjoyed the recognition, he found the task in action was a drag. Most of the creatures in his neighborhood had their merits, but worms were incredibly dull. "What do they *do* all day?" he would complain to his friends. "They eat dirt. They shit dirt. End of story." Still, they had to be respected for all the earth-softening they did. It was important for the comfort of the cicada world that the worms be encouraged to move through the substrate at their leisure. So, Simon respected them reluctantly.

That was a few years ago, during a time he now referred to as his Community Involvement period. Since then, he had grown more philosophical. His position with the WCD had afforded him a nicer burrow in a relatively new subdivision, and, more importantly, a disposable income. There wasn't much to buy underground—everyone wore the same uniform, internet was free—but you could still buy a book if you found one you liked. Simon Cicada found a lot of them he liked.

He started with Steinbeck, just to start somewhere. He read all the novels, then the short stories, underlining his favorite passages and later transcribing the underlined parts onto 3 × 5 cards, which he then posted on the wall of his room. After Steinbeck, he made a beeline for the Russians. Tolstoy he liked more than the fierier Dostoyevsky, but both broadened his insect mind, making him consider ways of being he hadn't thought of before. After the Russians, he spent a long time reading whatever was on the best-sellers list, but these books he found to be plot-driven and devoid of the character development he so enjoyed in his classics, so he went back to what he liked.

One day, after replacing a copy of Walker Percy's *The Moviegoer* on the shelf, he had a disturbing feeling. An itching feeling. Was he imagining it? He paused, resting his spiny brown foreleg on the bookcase and considering the possibilities. It's true that he was, by nature, something of a neurotic. And reading, while broadening his horizons, etc., had also made him a lot *more* neurotic. Maybe the itching was in his mind?

After a minute of being still, he knew. There was no doubt. His exoskeleton was itching like tree sap on a compound eye. Simon didn't like it. He didn't know what it meant, but he didn't like it at all.

Something like a slow panic began to burn inside him. He hurried across the floor of his room and through the tunnel over the tree root and around the Great Rock to his neighbor's house. His neighbor was a doctor; he would know what to do.

But when Simon Cicada knocked on the door, there was no answer. No one home. That was weird. The doctor was retired. He was always home.

Simon stood at the door of the empty burrow and thought about what this could mean. He had lived for thirteen years underground. It was all he knew. And for better or worse, life had been the same for so long that he had never considered the possibility that it might one day change. And now, suddenly and without warning, were two changes: the ever-present neighbor was gone and he himself was itching like he had never itched before.

Involuntarily, the tymbals on the sides of Simon's belly began to shiver. At another time, he might have cooly observed, "Ah, so this is how a cicada screams," but right now, observer and actor were one. The world was changing and Simon was terrified, and now he was screeching like a burned moth.

As he rushed headlong through the network of tunnels he and his kind had so painstakingly created over these thirteen years, he tried to reflect on what his books had told him. Circle of life, heroic descent, all that. But it was one thing to ponder a change from the comfort of one's room, a cup of sweetroot tea at one's side, and another entirely to be driven through your underground village by a maddening itch, the origins of which you don't understand. He was trying to escape, and he was looking for something at the same time, but he had no idea what. It was just a feeling, a terrible feeling.

When he finally arrived at the Centersquare he was greeted with such a scene as he had never beheld in his whole life. Every insect in his brood was there, chattering excitedly and hugging goodbyes and making like something wonderful was about to happen. Some of the cicadas were already climbing upward toward the tunnels that led to the Surface.

"What is going on?!" shouted Simon at the cicada nearest him. "I'm so afraid!"

The cicada, a lovely female with big red eyes, turned and said, "It's time for us to go! Isn't it exciting? We don't have to be nymphs any longer!"

"But I like being a nymph!" cried Simon. "I like it just fine! I don't want to go up there. It's scary, and I'll be all alone, and something will eat me."

"But," said the girl cicada, "You'll fly. And for the first time, you'll see the world and not just read about it. You were given eyes to see, and for your whole life, you've been hiding in darkness, waiting for this time. And now it's here! It's so exciting!"

But Simon wasn't excited. He was alarmed. This was too much change, and it was happening too quickly. He didn't want it. He wanted to sit in his burrow and sip tea and read books about love.

Meanwhile, the other cicadas were already disappearing into the Up Tunnels. The female with the red eyes was gone. It was happening quickly. The very ground was quivering with the great exodus of molting insects. He felt the shaking outside and the itching within. Simon Cicada wanted to go back home, to retrieve some special items. He couldn't think of what those would be, but there would be something. He just wanted to go *back*. Back to what was familiar, to what he knew. He wanted it more than he had ever wanted anything in his life. Oh, to go back to what was! Plus, the itching was making him *crazy.*

Suddenly, in the chaos of the fleeing cicadas, Simon heard something very quiet. It was the quietness of it that made him pay attention. It was a loud-quiet, a voice. The voice said, "You are free to do anything you want. You are free to go forward and free to resist. To go forward will be painful, to be sure, but the resisting will be worse."

In that moment, Simon Cicada's heart was broken in two. It was fear that did it. Like a hammer pounding a rock until it split. He was so afraid and yet he knew. He would never see his home again. He would never hold his favorite book or sip from his favorite cup. All the little passages he had written down would be left and gone forever. He would never visit the doctor. But he would go forward, even if it meant certain death. He would do what he was called to do.

As he made his way through the tunnel leading up to the surface, Simon understood that he had spent his life preparing for this moment. Preparing for the time when he would leave behind all the things he had thought were so important and begin his one-way climb toward the light, so frightening, so uncertain, so bright with possibility.

On his back and through the decay of his broken flesh, Simon Cicada felt the stirring of something he had never before known. Wings.

ACKNOWLEDGMENTS

Thank you to all the misfits, strangers, friends, and detractors who have helped me make these stories. Some of you were here at the beginning and still are, some of you took an early exit. Some appear in these pages explicitly (albeit with different names, mostly), some in spirit. A few of you had no idea I was even paying attention. Well I was. Special thanks to Denae Gaunce for spending that week in Sante Fe going through all the stories with me line by line and being just the right balance of mean and encouraging. Let's be honest, I wouldn't have done this without your help.

Thanks to the authors early on that made me see what stories can be: Beverly Cleary, Roald Dahl, the guy who wrote the Great Brain books. Not sure if it's okay to thank authors in these things but it's my book and I'm doing it anyway. You were the first to show me how words makes worlds. It was the best gift I ever got.

Thank you to my parents for whom some of these stories may have been difficult. Everyone I know adores you, Keegan and Kenna and me most of all. Sorry for all the dumb stuff I did, but I think it will be okay in the end. Also I want to say that when I think of marriages worth emulating, I can't think of many. Yours stands out. Thank you for loving each other.

I want to thank all of you who are part of my music, who come to the shows, who let me make music in your club, in your cd player, in your house. These stories are largely the result of the rambling life I have thus far lived, the mechanism of which has turned on the friendship and enablers of my musical efforts. Thanks too to the fellow musicians with whom I've shared cars, vans, rooms. Thanks for smiling through the parts when I was having a hard time being pleasant.

A special thank you to Stephanie Beard at Turner for pulling the trigger and being my first real friend and advocate in the book world. No matter what happens, I owe you a lot.

Thanks also: Todd Bottorff, Caroline Davidson, and everyone at Turner. Katie McDougall, Susannah Felts, Kendall Highnote and everyone at The Porch in Nashville. Julie Schoerke and the powerhouse team at JKS media. Thank you Parnassus Books for being bold and bright and savvy and dancing. And thank you to that grumpy couple at Henderson Books in Bellingham, Washington for making the wonderful used book store that pretty much shaped my twenties. All book people are good people.

Finally, thank you Danny Dalby for thinking of me when you found that stuffed piranha at the flea market. I was wrong. Most friendships are complicated.

CPSIA information can be obtained
at www.ICGtesting.com
Printed in the USA
LVOW04*0513141115
462558LV00006B/7/P